I LOOKED ALIVE

I LOOKED ALIVE I LOOKED ALIVE I

Gary Lutz

OOKED ALIVE **I LOOKED ALIVE**

BLACK SQUARE EDITIONS & THE BROOKLYN RAIL 2010

Cover image: *Profile, Harry Roseman* (1994)
Oil on canvas, 45 x 41 inches
Copyright © Catherine Murphy (American, 1946)
Courtesy Knoedler & Company, New York

Design by Shari DeGraw

The entries herein are works of fiction. Names, characters, places,
and incidents are the product of the author's imagination or have
been used fictitiously. Any resemblance to actual persons, living or
dead, as well as to actual events or locales, is entirely coincidental.

ISBN: 1-934029-07-6
ISBN 13: 978-1-934029-07-7

Black Square Editions and The Brooklyn Rail
are distributed by SPD:
Small Press Distribution
1341 Seventh Street
Berkeley, CA 94710
1-800-869-7553
orders@spdbooks.org   www.spdbooks.org

Contributions and checks should be made to:
The Brooklyn Rail
99 Commercial Street No. 15
Brooklyn, NY 11222

blacksquare@brooklynrail.org

to Gordon Lish
and
for *Anna* DeForest

CONTENTS

A WOMAN WITH NO MIDDLE NAME

I HAD NOT come through in either of the kids. They took their mother's bunching of features, and were breeze-shaken things, and did not cut too far into life.

They were out in the yard, often as not, standing childheartedly and hasteless near something barely coming up beyond the fence.

But had I at least put myself across in my wife? I had twenty years on her. They were packed down so hard on the two of us, those decades, that it was all but murder to get even so much as an arm moving concernedly away.

I should be saying what her draws were instead of what they drew me toward.

ONE DAY, in other words, I chose the toll road on my way home from work and pulled over at a rest stop. I began mixing with the men in the toilets there, tapping them for their hourly saps.

Stalls they were called, and how fitting, because they were structurally apt for delay, detainment, holding over. I started dashing off a private life for myself inside.

One afternoon I go in one and there's a hair kinkled up from the rim of the bowl, stuck. It's an upshooting thing that I pluck and take into freakful consideration.

I travel a little of its crinkled, coiling span.

Somebody tries the door, is not persistent enough.

From the next stall comes the beginning of a plea.

I go visit.

This one is keen-haired, wide-kneed. Wants me to piss justly but off-aimedly between his parted legs where he sits.

I'm not lacking a knack for anything this chummy with a scrawny, lopsided cock.

Then there's talk.

Him: Some days the whole world lags and withholds.

Me: Everything makes a point of taking itself down a peg.

Him: Other days, you see straight up through the hours to where things might still have a chance of getting started.

Once he's gone, I sit a little, wiped. Through the open rectangle beneath the door, I take note of the blind, dodgy society of passing shoes and trouser cuffs. Now and then there is a giveaway, interested pause.

The next one in has cleaned himself first at the sinks.

When I start on him, the hair on his arms is still wet, streaked flatly, linily, across the skin. By the time we part, it has gained back its upreach, its fluff.

My wife comes clarifiedly to mind:

My love for her has surely got to be *convex*.

I mean, there might as well be a dome I keep seeing put over it.

It's underneath, booming unharmed.

MY WIFE: the way, in bed, undressed, she bent the lower leg back against the upper one gave you, where they met in a line, the thin, shy, wibbling mouth of it. A dolphin it was, or a porpoise – whichever. She was good at getting forms and shapes to come out on her like that.

But I do not want to make her out to be anything other than a wife who mostly hoarded herself and now and again insisted on knowing something of the world's trickier wordings.

E.g.: *I got up on the wrong side of the bed.*

The bed, I tried explaining, is more widespread than either of us can ever have reason to hope to know. The whole mattressy vastness of it gets zoned and rezoned and terrained anew while you doze. Step off of it come morning and don't expect to be certain of what all you're deserting.

I pointed at sheets impressed topographically by our pokes, our tossings:

Empire after empire we had turned our backs upon.

THE ATTENDANT? There was sometimes more than one. I worked up a gaunt understanding with each. I explained my indisposition as a collapsion, an intestinovesical circumstance, that obliged me to make a prolonged, daily stop about halfway home. I was sorry to make their lives harder, even offered to fill out the cleanup-schedule checklist posted by the hand-dryers if they ever felt like blowing off their hourly rounds. How I marvelled at those charts, the narrow rectangles taking the day so completely to pieces.

Today a kid I figure for someone newly torn off—still fresh, I guess, from having the news finally broken to him. He's nervous but clean-breathing in a T-shirt relieved of sleeves. Just blond frizzle under his arms, rimmed by deodorantal chalk. I tell him that whoever she was, he'll be burying her beneath whichever one he'll have under him next.

What comes to hand is on the order of tears, only clingier, better condensed.

I place the taste: chlorine.

I go home and fish for compliments.

WHAT'S SAUCE for the goose is sauce for the gander.

We will both see need, I tell her, of sneaked flavorings and creams —worthful droplings pestered from whatever is hardest put on some other body.

That night a leg of hers shoots up in her sleep and keeps itself aloft, playing, I gather, at departure.

ONE EVENING I put in some time as the father and treat the kids to budget golf. We take to the welcome, vivid obstacles, the flimsy windmill, the slopping low waters of the moat. You don't get to pick your ball out of the final hole. It goes clanking down a pipe. This the kids decide is distress.

I find I favor the confectionary complexion of the boy. (The girl's trifling, offsprung body has already gone to the trouble of widening its pores.)

I ask after their friends. The girl names a quick, organized three. The boy doesn't come up with any. A look of annoyance looks tossed onto his face.

The migratory blemish on his arm has reached the gateway to the fingers. (But the fingernails are bright, baubled.)

The cigarette his sister finally shows me has gone much too long unlighted. (The tobacco has come unpacked. The thing sags in her lank grasp.)

Afterward, I drive them past the rest stop. I backtrack, then leave them with shallow, gaudy sodas while I drop in for my functions.

A few minutes and there's one close to me in age, a fearer first, then a negotiant, then an eye-closer certain of something coming to him. His slim face is a theater of twinges and tics, the strict hairs looking splintered into the chin. He takes some getting used to, and then my feelings for him thin.

A HOUSE is not a home.

It's just an unflattering brick-and-shingle apparatus for seeing to it that people get bulked into belittling intimacy on the un-lofty proppage of furniture.

Still, something big should have happened every time I dried myself with her towel. Smitches of her dead, departed skin should have held fast to my back, my arms.

I should have felt enlarged, defended.

THESE MEN—I knew what was inquirable about most of them, and I fetched it out: modicumal indoor data about the upbringing of their dogs, setbacks and obscurities in their livelihoods, milestones in their ungreatening associations with whoever might still have had the upper hand at home.

Then some of them wanted to have something on *me*. There were three memories I circulated, all slenderly accurate.

The first, and least excludable:

My parents hit the ceiling when they found out I had not been seeing a thing on the blackboard. (All along I had been reasoning that the teacher kept going to the board and turning his back on us just as a courtesy.)

Thus the rush-job eyeglasses: I got them strutted over my ears, and watched every face break out into unbeneficial linearities, crevices, pockings. A snug indefinitude fled the world. I saw what was written up front in chalk: the tilting, calculatory digits, the names of stars and states. That was thorough enough sorrow for me for weeks.

A FEW TIMES, though, I just sit in my car outside the place. A down-rolled window attracts eventual, diplomatic conversation. I invite the man in. He's deep-faced and deserving in his daintihood and modest designs. My hand joins his in his coat pocket, and then come tender knee-knocks, and in no time we are describing fundamentally the same faceful of spiteless, tolerative wife put to hazard at home. They're alike, these wives, down to the marriage marks along the stoutened back of the leg, the unshunning eyes. We're of one mind on it: eyes look better on a woman.

THEN A LATE afternoon. From the neighboring stall, an at-long-last, loud-whispered "Nor I you."

He leaves, is succeeded.

The new one clears his throat.

Then: "Fewer words were never spoken."

Then: "What are you thinking?"

I give my kids a thought: had I bled them white enough to start them out all right?

As for marriage, husbandhood, wife-having: I liked variety and novelty in how I was still not quite up to the task. I no longer pried into her body, but that night I made sure I took a felt-tip marker to her knee and darkened it with just abbreviations, things we both could see.

A.M., F.M. "Against me, for me," I said.

WWII. "Wuv wou too."

H2O. "Hate to overstay."

THE SECOND MEMORY I get passed around in the latrines?

The twenty years I was her senior, the years just before I flopped down on her—they had not lent themselves too steadily to duration.

The calendar kept troubling the seasons with three-day weekends. Enough of their minutes would get pressed together into one hour, then another, and at long last one day got itself driven through the next.

I seemed to be the one person always seen going out for the mail.

I was a notifyee.

Then I fell on vaguer days.

THEN ONE NIGHT it's finally her telling me.

No news is good news, I say.

"How wouldn't it have hurt?" she says.

I killed two birds with one stone, I say.

"Don't flatter yourself," she says. "They would've crashed into each other anyway."

The way to a man's heart is through his stomach.

"Only if you come up through the ass."

BUT I COUNT on every one of them to be at least privately, niggardly, beautiful. I count on even the most foul-browed and unfingerable to admit me to at least one beautiful place.

This one has blocky teeth, a beety face.

Hair frustrated forward into a dirty-blond surge.

A juvenility to the unmuscled upper arm.

I get almost all of him out into the open before I find it: hard by the ankle bone, the charm of a scar, a volant, darksome swash looking unsettled enough, I decide, to be ready to make the crossing from his body to maybe finally mine.

AND THE THIRD MEMORY?

It was only of what sleep had been like back when dreams still briefed me for the day ahead, instead of just shaking up what little the finished one had thrown my way.

"BUT SHOULDN'T WE be painting the town red?" my wife is the one to be saying one night. "Don't we look like people who would be so much better off painting the whole town red?"

We're already in bed, though, and through.

Then she pulls the monthly thing out from between her legs by the string that might as well be a fuse.

Daubs a little of the warm stickiness onto the back of my arm. Sparingly, but fidgetless in her thrift with it.

"Get your clothes on," she says, and throws on a robe.

In the car, her passenger, I am of course the one to keep holding it, and I am the one who folds.

CARRIERS

W ERE I TO KEEP talking about barely the one thing, which is that for too long a time I lived in the trouble between women and men without taking anywhere nearly enough of it for my own, I would humor myself at least as far as discovering, all over again, beyond example, that the thing to do with a man, the fittest way yet for a woman left like me to get a man put to rights, was to set him three, maybe four paces in advance of me on the sidewalk and let him block out what would otherwise have been my view of even more of the town—the sun-porched, shingle-thin enormity of where I was still hard up in the hours. How else to get it explained that I one day fell behind a slow-gaited man whose back was presented to me as a helpful column—a wall, practically—of broad-shouldered, long-skirted topcoat? For I walked as far as this man went, trick-stepping in back of him, letting the bulk of him give momentary concealment to a birdbath here, a mailbox there, or, farther off, samples of regional humanity, the women and measlier men, whom we could depend on to cross to the far side of the street at first sight of our staggered, our loose-coupled progress. By week's end, I had put myself permanently to the rear of this man, enrolled myself matrimonially in the confined violence by which he was taking the place out

of visibility, one piece at a time, for my sake alone. He had failing, aimless hair of a muddled gray already, and a well-founded
nose skewed just a trifle to the right, and an inclement complexion, and he brought a modest outlay of emotion to a house
I had already filled mostly with shelving—miles of it, I would
have then imagined, that ran like elevated tracks from room
to faraway room. I remember a year or so of sharp smells and
shared expenses and half-swallowed avowals, and then we were
sudden, slapdash parents of an eyesore son. Low birth weight,
premature, got up in cottons—not a girl at all. "He flatters you,"
the nurse said to my husband's face. "He favors you," the doctor
whispered shrewdly at mine. And: "I'm not just saying that." We
spent a couple of months on this infant, fetching affection from
its mouth, from the graspless, uncatching fingers, but it gave us
up, it gave out on us, it did not stick with us for long. The direc-
tor of the funeral wanted to have a word with me in a side room,
not the office they usually used. He was a short, honed-looking
man, condensed in his speech, and there was sordid hard candy
in the footed dish he kept pointing to. He said that people, left
to themselves, revolved in a very slow, a very limited circle of
feeling, and, oh, how he wished that to have been clumsily loved
could just this once be counted a life in itself. Then came a spoiling silence, and a silence following that, and finally he said, "I
should get you to the things." I let my face color for him just a
little, the way I now and then did for people in positions.

Words were a little looser now in the things I hardly said. You
will want to know whether we worked, my husband and I, and
the answer is an unemphasizing yes: we both had jobs, we both
kept books, but in different places, for different concerns.

There was a desk I went to, a back-office destination of con-
centrated gray, and as a person who looked kindly on all openings, I would admit my legs into the kneehole, then fall out of
my feelings long enough to nurse the numbers I worked with,
getting them to hold up or, with a pencil with extra-hard lead,
trapping them just beneath the surface of the ledgered page.

Whenever I looked away from them, I became less and less certain of the term, the longevity, of any "hello" I might have earlier fixed upon any of my co-workers – of how long the greeting would stay in force, how long until it had to be renewed, or updated, or varied – and I sent my gaze out onto a woman, a new one, at a wayside desk, and onto her sleeve, a short, side-slit one of rayon, and the way the flesh of the arm seemed to come washing down out of it, toward me. There was a defective hour toward the end of the workday when, elbow propped on desktop, I would let any little thing, whichever had worked its way up into my sight, come between my cheek and the flat of my hand. I would thus arrive home bearing the perishable impress of the twinned, concentric circles of a cellophane-tape refill, maybe, or just the trombone-slide tricksomeness of a jumbo paper clip.

Any other husband would have said, "Let me have a look at you."

Instead, I would have to shout, "What's stopping you then?"

But I had to remind myself that my husband came from a desk of his own, a desk that constituted itself, it's true, out of unoverlapping planes, plywood sectionings, splinty and unvarnished panels, that came ramping out at him and were held up, kept aloft, by the top rails of certain cast-off folding chairs of unrivalling heights. It was on this unhelpful surface that he fitted the numberings he was good at into preset stopgap calculations. There was a hole in the left pocket of his blazer (my fault again), and much of whatever was entered into it would get sent down into a second, more deepgoing pocket, whose lower limit was some overburdened stitchwork of lining that gave out just above the blazer's woolly inner hem. In this further pocket were pencils, a rainy-day dozen of them, that tunked against one another in sheltered and futile abundance.

So we worked, yes, and kept up the sneaky peace between us. But now and again life falls due on certain parts of persons, the most tampered-with parts, the ones best centered on us – or is this something we take a vote on now, too?

Because what came next I can get to come out civilly only in numbers:

1

He found a longer, a more dissenting way to lure himself homeward at night and started smelling, I was sure, of other men: their lonesome deodorants, their waning aftershaves.

2

He acquired the same narrow stripe of mustache I had been noticing on certain of the lesser local men. (The little hairs seemed needled into the upper lip.) He began taking fresh pains with his wardrobe. Everything he now wore smelled rainily of the iron.

3

At dinner one night, a tiny slip of a bracelet, thin as thread, stole down from under the cuff of his buttoned sleeve and sent a glimmer out over his plate.

4

"No going below the heart" was the line he started using to clear my arms and keep me on my toes.

5

His things came out of the medicine cabinet and vanished, one after another, into a toiletries bag he now favored on a makeshift shelf set high above the toilet. I went after it just the one time. The zipper made a fretty, testy, protesting sound, a little-sister version of the full-toothed aggrievance I kept hearing from the never-ending zippers of the garment bags, half-closetfuls of them, holding his clothes in shaming separation from mine.

6

Another night: a dinner of unplanned sandwiches away from the table, and a shift, a repositioning, of his leg brought the hem of his trousers a half-inch or so above the upper reaches of his sock. In the clearance I caught the sheeny meshwork of nylon.

7

Another night—one is never through enough with one's meal—
he called me "sisterfamilias," then placed a disaffiliating hand
over mine.

LOOK: IS IT only the question, all over again, of how to keep
yourself innovative emotionally when men have easier, dicky
stuff all their own?

Because this took place back when soda still came in grave,
shapely bottles—the slender ones, violently unsteady once you
withdrew one from the carton and stood it up at last on the table.
In this case, it was a towerlike and topplesome sixteen-ouncer
that brought a fresh unrest not to the kitchen table (how could
I eat?), but to an outlying one, a step table, a side table, the one I
strewed with my collectings, my pertainings, my daily securities
of tissue and receipts. I remember worrying my hand around
the bottle and bringing the thing close enough to my face to see
how chipped the glass might be around the lip. But it was the
carton itself, the carrier the soda had come in, the host, with its
eight flimsily flapped and tabbed cardboard compartments, that
gave me ambition.

I ran out to one of those office-supply places and brought back
a cheap little printing outfit, the kind that sets you to tweezering
tiny rubber letters the color of brick into gutterlike slots grooved
into a little wooden holder that soon enough finds itself, meanly,
at the ends of your fingers. I pried open the stinking stamp pad,
then stressed my message ("There are two of us to one of you")
and the petty digits of our phone number onto the little dibbled
squares of scratch paper that had come with the kit. Then I put
myself into the car again and, making a tour of the supermarkets,
shoved the paper squares into the compartments of the soda cartons, one to a carton, the outermost cartons on whatever shelf
was at eye level of the adult, useless, stand-alone male.

Then of course days, the minutes pounding around in every
one of them: you wait, you wait, the phone rings finally one
night, and at the other end there is a voice at first untoned and

already in decline, then clearing itself afresh, the words barely filling out what has to make itself get said, and then my own contribution – the crisp specifics of time, of address, and of what to watch out for on the way. Because there are people who cannot wait to be met by the airs of anyone else's house – the private, longtime vapors of the human catastrophe differently contained.

Or there's at least one such person.

Except he called back and said we should meet him instead outside a bakeshop we were to recognize, he promised, by the unsoiled upstretch of its blond brick in a close-by town that was otherwise all smudged, charmless horizontals. We thought we were early, and then a man came out, taller than either one of us, but knuckled-under-looking, all silent treatment, and he brought to his face an expression – in answer, I supposed, to one of my own – that put him nicely along, I decided, in lives he had yet to lay eyes on. Wastes of hair, curls the color of iodine, showed between the collar blades of his shirt, and I watched my husband get himself taken with the man, or take his part at least a little. There was a tiny paper bag in the man's hand, and without having to dip his fingers into it, and by means, instead, of clever manipulations of the bag from without and beneath, he worked a cookie up into the throat of it and pinched off the rest of the contents. It was a crumblish sugar cookie I reached for and took one bite of before passing it along, festively, to my husband. The man had still yet to speak a word, but my husband and I must have felt spoken to completely, for we let the man guide us across the street to the car he kept pointing to, and we let ourselves be put into finicky automotivation with him, my husband of course up in the front.

The voice that finally broke away from the man was hard on words but got it put far enough out into speech that he was strapped for companionship, and the reason was always for a number of reasons, naturally, but the one he was offering us was that he was one half, the more spacious half, of a marriage to a woman who wasn't just anybody but who was hardly a shop-

lifter, either, though she had an overactive feel for merchandise —
juvenile cosmetics, mostly — and knew how easily the motions of
their molecules could be made to shut down until the lipsticks,
the compacts and applicators, suffered a persuasive, deserving
absenteeism from the pegboard wall of the store, then declared
themselves with renewed materiality in the pockets of her coat.
"Life isn't apportioned equally into people" was the line he said she
made good use of on the store detectives, and were we ourselves
willing to go along with him that far?

"Or it can go the other way around for a change, can't it?" the
man said. "You two can be the ones asking *me* how it's any fairer
to keep saying it's the woman who puts out when in fact she's
the one taking it all in? It's the man who ends up *minus*? He's the
one you see leaking all over the place?"

This voice of the man's sounded messy, squirky, from disuse,
and in the rearview mirror I enjoyed a pretty decent view of the
mouth it was coming from: I could see past the settlement of
crowns up front to the slummy molars, packed high with fillings, and now and then get a glimpse of the gumline, a corpus-
cular dirty red. I was probably making saliva lap against my own
gums in response.

But the man raised himself up on the subject of his grown
children, a couple of "undressed, knucklekneed housebounds,"
and how they landed their legs on each other, and how, the way
some unfortunates could throw their voices, these two had now
started throwing their sight, taking in one person, toiling away
at his face, while appearing all the while to be giving full, bratty
regard to somebody else entirely. The man rushed us past where
he had put them up in a place of their own: some scarcely win-
dowed blockwork the hard height of two stories. But he was
already remarking how you kept seeing more and more drivers
advancing through traffic with the left arm stretched to full
length out the side window. This was not to be taken for the
stage business of lazing an arm around in the breeze or test-
ing the sky for drops; this was high-minded dirty work — putting

one tensed section of the body as far out of touch with the rest of it as you could manage in passing.

"But you two," he said, "you kids aren't up too far on any high horse yet? You're still new to the problem? You can see your way to where I am practically half the time?"

He brought the car to a stop in a garage whose door was already wide open, and we followed him through a breezeway to a kitchen, then up some stairs and past a diversity of doors, all shut, and into the room with the comprehensive bed.

Then there was big talk, all the man's, about how some people spotted easily and others could not even be bothered to wash their hands.

In the powder room off to the side, I had to make up my mind between how mushy the cake of soap seemed underneath and how smooth and solid it still looked on top. Then it was either a lank hanging of towel trapped halfway through a hoop on the wall or just tissues I could tear from a tight boxful on a shelf. I had always been rough on whatever I shuddered to think, had always lived a little in advance of my feelings, had always exempted myself from much of whatever I might have found reason to have to touch, so what else needed doing other than keeping myself reminded that to think a thing through meant only hollowing it out, letting it cave in, seeing it to a successful collapse?

By the time I reached the bed, the man had already tugged most of the dayshine out of the blinds. There was the worsening sound of persons parting themselves, sorry-leggedly, from underclothes, then my husband going for what was posted on the man at midbody, taking it into his confidence, and I going unfavoredly for the leftover mouth, which was luridly elaborative while I was still on my way but then went vague altogether once I got there.

Because this was just once more only me at my least: getting one person drawn through another, cutting myself dead in the two of them.

CHAISE LOZENGE

MONTHS ACCUMULATED. I was nowhere nearer female.
The look I had been shooting for? You've seen it on girls
who are studious about unpivotal things, on older young wom-
en looking cornered already, pushing forward in unelegiac life.

Then the tresses came off. Bracelets no longer plinked on my
wrist. No more nail polish, not even the clear. A moderate over-
haul of the vocabulary—purging of qualifiers and the airier
adjectives.

By this point, I was living entirely in effigy. The city made a
yellow amoeboid splash on the road map of the state. Sleep was
choppy, unproductive. My car was getting keyed. Lots of hastened
engravery on the side panels, the trunk.

I chippered up my mumping tenor with telephone-solicitor
effects, taught myself to space out my swallows, breezed through
screening interviews for temp positions as telefundraiser, tele-
activist, appointment-setter. I would get hired, pile my self and
scripts and fizzes into a cubicle, crook my long legs into a sleep-
defeating stance, then get called down after the first monitored
exchange.

I had soon made all the lateral moves allowable in my lonesome lines of employ. "Suppose we gave you some bad news,"

a supervisor ventured one afternoon. "You're sure there would be someone for you to really tell it to?"

Once it was only a Tuesday, but I felt already deep in the week, through with so much that still was new, untried. In my father's house I had a room to myself but did not reign in it. My father was always at home. Beyond that, he was no nonpareil.

You can buy just one fork, I found out.

Or you can take the other view: that cunt had to be the contraction of something, and somebody just forgot to pop the apostrophes in.

I.e., c'u'n't = could not.

Because I couldn't.

"Meaning now you can?" one of them – the women – was first to ask. People talked about the airs this one gave herself, and I sometimes did do her the favor of picturing an essenced mist adrift above her head, some ozone she alone had. I should have been able to bat it away, get it to settle over somebody else, let it drizzle down onto this or that walkaway replacement, who would enrich me or finish me off.

The next one went about in low-hanging sweaters and was a cherisher, true, but there was always something probationary in her regard for whatever she cherished. There was a fine-lined signature of hair on the backs of her hands.

Then my father's heart got backed up. Things weren't getting into it, or out of it afterward – there was one stoppage or another. I should know the words.

When he died, I handled everything with the local paper. I sat at the kitchen table with the dummy résumé I had only weeks earlier freed from a library book. I beefed up his education, work history, community service. The obit ran the next day with just one misprint: "chaise lozenge."

After the burial, a buffet at my mother's. My sister was there with her peer – not the one she married but the woman one. They insisted I come stay with them. I became known as the perfect guest because of how good I got at sponging mouth-marks off the glasses.

PEOPLE SHOULDN'T HAVE TO BE
THE ONES TO TELL YOU

H E HAD a couple of grown daughters, disappointers, with regretted curiosities and the heavy venture of having once looked alive. One night it was only the older who came by. It was photos she brought: somebody she claimed was more recent. He started approvingly through the sequence. A man with capped-over hair and a face drowned out by sunlight was seen from unintimate range in decorated settings out-of-doors. The coat he wore was always a dark-blue thing of medium hang. But in one shot you could make out the ragged line of a zipper, and in another a column of buttons, and in still another the buttons were no longer the knobby kind but toggles, and in yet another they were not even buttons, just snaps. Sometimes the coat had grown a drawstring. The pockets varied by slant and flap-work. The father advanced through the stack again. His eye this time was caught in doubt by the collar. A contrastive leather in this shot, common corduroy in that one, undiversified cloth in a third. And he was expected to make believe they were all of the same man? He swallowed clumsily, jumbled through the photographs once more.

"But you'll still have time for your sister?" he said.

Her teeth were off-colored and fitted almost mosaicwise into the entire halted smile.

A FEW NIGHTS LATER, the younger. A night class was making
her interview a relation for a memory from way back and then
another from only last week. He was not the best person to be
in recall, but he thought assistively of a late afternoon he had sat
at a table outside a gymnasium and torn tickets off a wheel one at
a time instead of in twos and threes for the couples and three-
somes. He had watched them file arm-in-arm into the creped-up
place with a revived, stupid sense of how things ought to be done.
A banquet? A dance? He never stayed around for things.

He saw his words descend into the whirling ungaieties of her
longhand.

"And one from just last week?"

Easier.

At the Laundromat, he had chosen the dryer with a spent fab-
ric-softener sheet teased behind inside it. He brought the sheet
home afterward to wonder whether it was more a mysticization
of a tissue than a denigration of one. It was sparser in its weave
yet harder to tear apart, ready in his hand when unthrobbing
things of his life could stand to be swabbed clean.

(He watched his daughter wait a considerate, twingeing minute before she set down the tumbler from which she had been
sipping her faucet water.)

"Your sister's the one with the head for memory," he said. "You
ever even once think to ask her?"

MOST NIGHTS, the man's hair released its oils into the antima-
cassar at the back of his chair. The deepening oval of grease could
one day be worth his daughters' touch.

He got the two of them fixed in his mind again.

The older went in for dolled-up solitude but was better at bat-
ting around the good in people. Her loves were always either six
feet under or ten feet tall because of somebody else.

The younger was a rich inch more favored in height, but slower of statement. Men, women, were maybe not her type. But she
was otherwise an infatuate of whatever you set before her—even

the deep-nutted cledges of chocolate she picked apart for bits of skin.

They had tilted into each other early, then eased off, shied aside.

THEN THEY were wifely toward him for a night, poising curtains at his streetward windows, hurrying the wrinkles out from his other good pants, running to the bathroom between turns at his dirt. The older holding the dustpan again, the younger the brush—a stooped, ruining twosome losing balance in his favor.

They were on the sofa afterward, each with a can of surging soda.

"Third wheel," he said, and went into his bedroom to sit. Were there only two ways to think? One was that the day did not come to you whole. It was whiffled. Things were blowing out of it already. Or else a day was actually two half-days, each half-day divided into dozenths, each dozenth corrugated plentifully into its minutes. There was time.

He sat, stumped.

When he looked in on them again, they had already started going by their middle names—hard-pressed, standpat single syllables. Barb and Dot.

THE NEXT COUPLE of nights he kept late hours, pulling his ex-wife piecemeal out of some surviving unmindedness. The first night it was only the lay of her shoulders.

On the next: the girlhood browniness still upheld in her hair—a jewelried uprisal of it.

The souse of the cologne she had stuck by.

Budgets of color in her eyelids.

The night it was the downtrail of veins strung in her arms, he had had enough of her for him to reach at least futilely for the phone.

It was the younger's number he dialed.

It was a different, lower voice he brought the words up inside of. She had never been one to put the phone down on a pausing stranger.

"People shouldn't have to be the ones to tell you," he said.

ONE NIGHT, he went over their childhoods again. Had he done nearly enough?

Their mother had taught them that you can ask anybody anything, but it can't always be "Do I know you?"

That you had arms to bar yourself from people.

That you had to watch what you touched after you had already gone ahead and touched some other thing first.

That the most pestering thing on a man was the thing that kept playing tricks with how long it actually was.

For his part, he had got it across that a mirror could not be counted on to give its all. Should they ever need to know what they might look like, they were to keep their eyes off each other and come right to him. He would tell them what was there. In telling it, he put flight and force into the hair, nursed purpose into the lips, worked a birthmark into the shape of a slipper.

Each had a room to roam however she saw fit in either fickleness or frailty.

Rotten spots on the flesh of a banana were just "ingrown cinnamon."

The deep well of the vacuum cleaner accepted any puny jewelry they shed during naps.

The house met with cracks, lashings.

They walked themselves to his chair one day as separates, apprentices at the onrolling household loneliness. The older wanted to know whether it was less a help than a hindrance that things could not drop into your lap if you were sitting up straight to the table. The younger just wanted ways to stunt her growth that would not mean spending more money.

When they were older, and unreproduced, he figured they expected him to start taking after them at least a little. So he now and then let his eyes slave away at the backs of his fingers in the manner of the younger. He raised the older's keynote tone of gargly sorrow up as far into his voice as it deserved when it came time again to talk about his car, any occult change in how the thing took a curve.

SOME NIGHTS he saw his ex-wife's face put to fuming good use on each of theirs. His failings? A waviness around all he felt bad about, a slovenry mid-mouth. Before the layoffs: timid, uncivic behaviors that went uncomprehended. (Tidy electrical fires, backups downstairs, wastepaper calculations off by one dimmed digit.)

From where they had him sitting, to see a thing through meant only to insist on the transparency within it, to regard it as done and gone.

But adultery? It was either the practice, the craft, of going about as an adult, or there had been just that once. Poles above the woman's toilet had shot all the way up to the ceiling, hoisting shelves of pebble-grained plastic. The arc of his piss was at least a suggestion of a path that thoughts could later take. He went back to the bed and found her sitting almost straight up in her sleep. Her leg was drawn forward: a trough had formed between the line of the shinbone and some flab gathered to the side. It needed something running waterily down its course. All he had left in him now was spittle.

At home afterward: unkindred totes and carryalls arranged in wait beside the door. He poked into the closest one to see whose clothing it might be. His fingers came up with the even-glow plush and opponency of something segregatedly hers. A robe, or something in the robe family.

ONE NIGHT he paid a visit to the building where the two of them lived on different floors. First the older: buttons the size of quarters sewn at chafing intervals into the back panels of what she showed him to as a seat. He had to sit much farther forward than ordinarily. He gave her money to take the younger one out for a restaurant supper. "How will I know what she likes?" she said.

Then two flights up to the younger, but she was on the phone.
A doorway chinning bar hangered with work smocks blocked
him from the bedroom. The bathroom door was open. Passages
of masking tape stuck to the plastic apparatus of her hygiene had
been left uncaptioned. Everything smacked of what was better
kept to herself. When she got away from the phone, he gave her
money to pick something nice out for her sister. "But what?" she
said. "You've known her all your life," he said. "But other than
that?" she said.

NO SOONER did he have the two of them turning up in each
other's feelings again than his own days gave way underneath.

The library switched to the honor system. You had to sign the
books out yourself and come down hard when you botched their
return shelving. (He gawked mostly at histories, portly books
full of people putting themselves out.) He recovered a gorge of
hair from the bathroom drain and set it on the soap dish to pros-
per or at least keep up. There were two telephone directories for
the hallway table now—the official, phone-company one and the
rival, heavier on front matter, bus schedules, seating charts. You
had to know where to turn. He began breaking into a day from
odd slants, dozing through the lower afternoon, then stepping
out onto the platform of hours already packed beneath him. It
should have put him on a higher footing. He started collecting
sleeveless blouses—"shells" they were called. Was there anything
less devouring that a woman could pull politely over herself?
The arms swept through the holes and came right out again, un-
squandered. He tucked the shells between the mattress pad and
the mattress and barged above them in his sleep.

THE YOUNGER stopped by with an all-occasion assortment of
greeting cards from the dollar store. She fanned them out on the
floor so that only the greetings would show.

"Which ones can't I send?" she said.

"What aren't you to her?" he said.

"I'm not 'Across the Miles.'"

"Mail that when you're at the other end of town, running errands."

THEN THE MOVIE HOUSE in his neighborhood reduced the ticket price to a dollar. It was a frugal way to do himself out of a couple of hours. He followed the bad-mouthing on-screen or just sat politely until it was time to tip the rail of the side door.

He became a heavier dresser, a coverer.

The older called to say that while the younger was away, she had sneaked inside to screw new brass pulls into the drawer-fronts of her bureau.

"It'll all dawn on her," she said.

BEFORE THE WEEK wore out, the two of them came by together one night, alike in the sherbety tint to their lips, the violescent quickening to the eyelids. Identical rawhide laces around their necks, an identical paraphernalium (something from a tooth?) suspended from each. Hair toiled up into practically a bale, with elastics. High-rising shoes similar in squelch and hectic string-age. They were both full of an unelevated understanding of something they had noticed on TV—a substitution in the sched-ule. He had noticed it too. It hadn't improved him.

They were holding hands.

Each finger an independent tremble.

He had to tell them: "This is not a good time."

How much better to get the door shut against them now!

His nights were divided three ways. This was the hour for the return envelopes that came with the bills. The utilities no longer bothered printing the rubrics "NAME," "STREET," "CITY, STATE, ZIP" before the lines in the upper-left corner. The lines were yours to fill out as you wished.

Tonight: electric.

_____

_____

_____

He wrote:
Who sees?
Who sees?
Who sees?

THE NIGHT his car had to be dropped off for repairs, the older one offered to give him a ride home. He faced a windshield-wiper blade braced to its arm by garbage-bag ties. Come a certain age, she was saying, you start thinking differently of the people closest to hand. You dig up what you already know, but you turn it over more gently before bringing it all the way out. It might be no more than that she catches a cold at every change of the seasons. But why had it taken you this long to think the world of it?

He started listening to just the vowelly lining in what she said.

He skipped the casing consonants that made each word news.

It was carolly to him, a croon.

THE DAUGHTERS had wanted their ceremony held in the lunchroom where they worked. Other than him, it was only women who showed—a table's worth of overfragrant, older co-workers. The officiating one, the day supervisor, first wanted to run down her list of what she was in no position to do. It was a long, hounding list of the "including but not limited to" type. (This was not "espousage"; it was not "conjuncture"; it was "not in anywise matrimoniously unitudinal.") Then she turned to the daughters and read aloud from her folder to steepening effect that no matter where you might stand on whether things should come with time, it was only natural for you to want to close up whatever little space is left between you and whoever has been the most in your way or out of the question all this long while, and let a line finally be drawn right through the two of you on its quick-gone way to someplace else entirely. Nobody was twisting your arm for you to finish what you should have been screaming your lungs out for in public since practically day one.

The kiss was swift but depthening.

Then the reception. He was a marvel for once, waving himself loose from the greetings and salutes every time he realized anew that they were intended for the person beside him, or behind.

I HAVE TO FEEL HALVED

I

WE HAD TO SIT for an annual review at work, but the catch was that there were sliding criteria, standards unstable from one assessment period to the next, so I would usually be told that my voice on the phone sounded like a voice still slushy with sleep, or that there were things my co-workers felt they couldn't exude with me around, or that I extended my hand to clients as if awarding it to them; and I would get referred to a large-pored lady down a lonely hallway or to an intake person at a societal-arts building across the boulevard, once to just an eye doctor who spooked the examination room with floatings of milky light and blew onto my eyelids, then tried to atone.

2

OTHER THINGS weren't firming either. Word was that as a man you were expected to make the jump to women, but I was lunking through late middle age, my even spongier fifties, and living with a man younger by decades. Whatever I felt for him must have been way out of balance or all too little all the same.

It went unrecouped.

My heart kept bullying me into letting people like him pull anything.

3

I HAD FOUND him in an onlookers' bar on a short street that squinted off an avenue. This was in the extremity district. He was got up in some rayon trashery with three-quarter sleeves, a girl's slippery belt, fingernails flashened. I was a workingman after work after all. I menaced myself with examinations of his manner, his spruce, unperspiry practice of himself.

I sent out a hand, let my fingers pile themselves onto his.

Neither beer nor mints on his breath. (Maybe traces of merest salading.)

He pointed dimly to some further indefinite figure on the dance floor.

"Let me go finish a good-bye."

4

SOME NIGHTS my young man spoke up in his sleep—mostly solemnities, sometimes mostly spitten slang.

He slept in the bed and I slept in the chair next to the bed, or he slept on the floor and I slept endways along the foot of the bed (this thus left most of the bed available and bereft), or each of us slept on the floor at either side of the bed, or he slept in the chair and I did without sleep with throes in my stomach, gratings in my skull.

The bed had started out as just a mattress and a frame on casters, but it had then become a formal summit of sorts, unwelcoming heights of some kind, as a bed sometimes must whenever two persons are said to be close.

The bedclothes were of a faded, jumpy purple plaid. They looked unlikely to envelop.

And the chair—the chair was in fact only one of those valet chairs, the kind with a trouser hanger bolted to the highest of the back slats. The seat was a lid you could lift. I stored things in the hopper underneath:

Some quarter-socks of his, long unlaundered, looking now like pouches, meaningly unfilled.

Rimpled empty packets of those concise, hard-cased chocolates he had esteemed for a week.

A swidge of his hair, lifted once from trimmings in the sink.

Mornings, he would go off to work in curio retail I knew not
exactly where.

5

A HASHY COMPLEXION, hair pluffy and unmastered, a blush in
bare arms barely offered — some days there was no bouquet to be
made of him.

Other days I felt a sexual concern.

6

AN ACCELERATING metabolism meant he needed starches within arm's reach — pillowy regional bagels, pretzels sugared in their
contortions.

The next month: a diet of practically milkless milk, slabbed or
crumble-pattied substitutes for everything else.

The coffee he demanded was coffee ounced out into bags ex-
pensively by hand.

These were luxuriations funded by a mother who mothered
him skeptically and kept narrowing her love until it was a thing
that gored.

7

I NEVER got the truth out of him, only things peeled off from
the truth, things the truth had shed.

Then one night a woman, young, was asking for him at the
door. She was scrawny and obscure in some sleeveless construct.
Matte-black hair hung from her head like curtains stiffened.

The face? Homely, abrupt. The nose? Respecified with cosmetics.

There was fight, though, in the eyes.

I did not have to ask who she was, only what she thought she
was doing.

"I am asking for him back."

8

ANOTHER NIGHT, another visitor at the door: a regretful man almost my age but more hit-or-miss in his panic: hands so swooping and opposed to each other, he seemed to be crossing himself out as he spoke: "He won't be needing the rest of his clothes?"

9

THIS WAS a lean apartment that threw itself out notionally over one side of a garage, though the garage wasn't mine to use. The place – there were three divisions of it, which you had to go ahead and count as rooms – was lengthwise unrealistic, but I lived with him within reason.

One day got chocked into the next: there was a blockiness to time, like a month's evident rectangulation on a calendar tacked fast to a wall.

His mother and stepfather made the trip aggressively from a metropolis of stone lawns and unhumid heat. They looked me over for signs that a life by my side would mean years lopped off his future.

These were unpleased people in airplane attire.

They could see nothing cerulean in me.

10

BESIDES, his teeth always clicked at the instant he fell asleep. He rioted quickly inward, and the next morning would wake up sore, bitten, bruised, infuriated. There was always an ache broiling behind a knee or a dream to be repudiated straightaway.

He must have valued me as somebody valuing him, for anything on his body accorded itself to something on mine, we matched in every fashion, but I had carnal recourse to him only rarely, and, even then, I never could go through with it, because it would have been only for minutes. I would have been only filler.

11

A JOB LIKE HIS — I knew the trouble it could take to get one hour jointed to another until you had an afternoon finishedly articulated.

After work, he travelled among other vague-waisted young men of temperament in taverns and tinderbox cabarets. He was allowed a happy hour or one hour of costlier socializing thereafter.

I am sure he danced and in the gaps between dances compelled a hand of his onto an unsturdying, neighbory shoulder and rested in restrooms after initiatives. I am sure he did whimsical things to make tears teem when he brought up how nippy it was at home, and how the laminated note taped to the thermostat counseled him to keep his prettily vagrant, bashable hands off.

He would come back to me with things written in sentiment on his wrist — e-mail whereabouts, mostly, or telephone integers already blearing.

12

HE HATED IT when it was the first of the month, and he hated it worse when it was a month that was no more.

The mail seldom brought him to satisfaction.

He could count to ten in different rampant tongues.

He kept his shaving ephemera, his quiver of tweezers, in a little trolley on the skirted table beside the sink.

The frontiers of this sink held toners and tinters vesselled pricily, effervescers by the jugful, cologne in a bullet-shaped bottle that I feared, had I brought the thing to my nose, would stink bitterly and forgivably of his ass, because his ass could hold its own among the presented openings of this world.

13

I HAD grown up in an outlying county of unfarmed farmland, shantied ridgeways.

Childhood was precisely the word, because I rose through those first years as if cowled, blindered.

How could "the country" be both the sticks we were living in and the state-laden, encompassing nation? The teacher pointed to an engulfing dictionary banished to a swively stand. I stayed unhugely in my seat.

Then middle school, high school, a back-facing junior college —none of it came to magnitude in me, either.

I thus drove myself to this guttery midget city for the gropery possible wherever people went drastic in numbers.

14

HE TOOK ALONG everything he owned even if storming out only for the weekend, or maybe he entrusted it all to a rental crypt somewhere, and I would turn the place upside down and prospect even the trash until I found something fortunate of his touch. Once it was a box of photo corners, those tiny, gummed triangles you licked to position snapshots squarely and evidentiarily onto the pages of an album, in this case a "presentation" album he had presented to his mother, double page after double page of us in poses of germane separation, never the two of us in the same picture, not even a long-ranging shadow to intimate that the other one of us was of degenerate consequence just outside the frame.

My signature mood was a maneuvering tenderness that bears forgetting.

15

HE WAS NOT THE FIRST, this one, and the second still wrote to me all the time, pressuredly typed letters and notes, printouts and packed follow-ups, paragraphs crammed over the sentiment panels of greeting cards, but the words seemed caged in what he wrote, not free to mean much of anything, and I did not show these to my partner, my match, my counterpart, who anyway was not a reader or even much of a listener to things read out loud, though he was a talker, unless by talking we mean the way I talk, which is not the way I am hoping to have finally spoken here.

16

AND THE FIRST ONE?

The way his name broke itself out of the alphabet and could barely be held to its spelling: it queered the mouth that pronounced it.

He was laid up the while I knew him, but his symptoms lacked a guiding disease.

17

MIDDLE OF THE WEEK, a pissiness at work again, and a suspicion that my features were not entirely concerted in their paining expression of same.

Then an unenjoyed, prettified doughnut creaming ever so little.

Then my young man called to give me some guff about a shirt. (It is said, isn't it, that you "make" love because it's otherwise not really there?)

The afternoon afterward got pursed with a worry first about an incisor (its glint was gone; it was no longer situated so stalwartly in the gums), then one about my car: the engine of late was letting out a mystic gibberish before it turned over. The papers I was supposed to be approving had the tread of someone's flatting intelligence on every clause. The matter had been trampled something terrible.

I tend to take notes when my reading fails me, and then I pleat each page of notes. I fold it all up, make tears until I've got practically a tulip. Then I go next door to the vending-machine nook for whatever is most orangely galore.

18

HE BOUGHT strainers, graters, spoon rests, corers, and filled shelf-papered drawers with still more, but we ate out at his daily insistence, though he scarcely ate—and the unforked entrées, things fruit-fringed and unpleasant of scale, got themselves committed to take-out canisters by waitresses severe in the wrist.

He had had a chandeliered childhood, I have made delay to mention, and had grown up trading spectral affections with grandaunts, letting great-uncles pant and prevail.

19

HE HAD left a roommate for me, or so he claimed, and their room, once he was gone from it, had rebounded by calling insects and rodents out of its walls—long-sequestered, veteran roaches, mostly, that now gave a syncopation to countertops and floorboards.

The roommate took to wearing overshirt over overshirt, and came down with a raucous, blistery sickness that brought him closer to the door of some other ill.

It was a door extant only in fits. Its existences were equivocal.

The door to the room, though, had photos, Polaroids, push-pinned to its backside. A house-calling doctor, a stockpot of a man with a satchel, told him to take them down or he would have to do it himself.

In these photos my young man was even younger and more abusive in his every sign of life: the steep features of the stoutened face, the fluke mole on the right cheek, a stricture already in the eyes, veins awriggle on the backs of the hands, the snippy hair on the knuckles—

But the roommate pulled through. There were days, weeks, of feeling plugged up with recovery. Then came elongating gurgulations in his sleep, unmotivated stiffenings of his dick all the standstill day.

He was soon directing himself retributively at girls.

He gave them the most disorganizing of attentions.

People knew this man later only for his cologne. It was a cologne that didn't hit you all at once—a citric breeziness at first, then an implication of other, less placeable fruits, and then it would strike a scolding afternote, then just as suddenly leave off, and you would be smelling matter-of-factly of only yourself, only more publicly now, and uncoverable.

20

BUT WHETHER it was my lonesomeness hosting his or the other way around, I felt his momentary devotions, or I felt belted to him and no more.

He was twenty-two years my junior, my miniature.

My life to come had come to be a wee thing.

And my hearing was practically shot. Sometimes it was only the vowels that reached me.

They came out of his mouth like pastels.

21

EVEN SO, he did not know enough about many things, but he veneered his ignorance with guidances from TV. (Hold your breath ten times during a tornado. Never feed your fish if you're feeling cross.) I was a radio hound, attentive to head-case polemics on the talk stations, though I never called in, and I was plenished with grammarless dire data from the daily paper, but it was in a leaflet reaching me physically through the mails that I first learned of a utopian procedure called "prostate milking of the semen" —fingerings of the gland, conducted rectally and by partner, that promised release without *release*. You felt nothing from your surge.

It was thus we expressed any bodily regard for each other those dashing months that dashed year.

22

AS A RULE, I kept a couple of friends, one of each, a filmy-eyed woman and a boggling fellow who tidied law offices overnight. I had known them when they were the demolitionary darlings of their crowd, but they were tamed, absolving people now.

The woman still had that voice that kept boiling right out at you.

Her hair had gone gruff.

As for the man, you couldn't always get him to show his face.

He was the more departing of the two, always putting words to your wave.

(He was often taken for a messenger.)

Both were all ears for my unracing earfuls. I must have told them enough and then finally enough.

Their refrain these days was: "Welcome to no club."

23

OR HE SPENT a lot of time exulting in the tub. His soaps were kept sleeved between soaks. I wanted to be clean in his manner, but water was never to be my element. I used a dry shampoo and a chunk deodorant and powdered myself many times over before I drove to work and sat up straight to the desk to get my lower body relievingly removed from the rest of me.

I had to feel halved.

The desk had come with a floor protector beneath it and a desk dictionary, not the household or college kind. The front matter boasted that the light thrown on the words defined therein was a light appropriate solely to the immediacies and sight lines of to-day's office backdrop. But when you poked your way to the definitions themselves, you were nowhere closer to things at all. Nothing was getting called what it was. You apparently had to look to your dreams for that, but to dream you first had to fall fast asleep, and I was not sleeping, not even when I was dead to the world.

24

THOSE BLACKOUTS and fast little faints of his—I assured him that they were just his verdict on me for that day alone.

Those pocks and pittings I could explain, too: life had bitten tinily away at him out of a hungering no unmonstrously different from mine.

I gave him mouthfuls of the like; I consoled; I rubbed his feet, which were narrow, tidy-toed, unpungent feet; and I did his laundry one item at a time to give full detergentive concern to

its petite but worldly dirts; and I seized on every chipped and
discolored thing that came up out of his vocabulary when he
talked his emptying talk on the phone.

25

MY FAMILY — I was barely gatherable with them for milestone
birthdays, anniversaries soothed over with reasons because. Life
had always pointed us away from each other. But I sometimes
went home just for the day, or maybe just the long and short of
a morning.

My mother liked to let a ringing telephone ring itself out in
tribute.

It was only things from far off that came out of her bowels.
She considered herself a conduit.

She preferred a footstool to a chair, and wore one pair of
glasses over another to get superior definition.

My father would circle almost anything at the back of a magazine. There was knowledge that jutted out of him oddly or forked
itself unwanted into your brain. A cancer meandered in him.

And I had a sister still living at home: eyelids detailed darkly,
and breasts alert even under those rolling sweaters, and always
an arm coming toward you with a glut of bracelets, and a mouth
that slanted actively when there were things to ask of you, things
to be more mum about.

The talk was generally without tenor.

The voice, no surprise, was sheer.

In sum: Father, Mother, Sister, Self: the four of us now and then
grouping ourselves genially around some cousin's graduating
niece, or contributing signatures to a gala kind of get-well card.

The extended family was exactly that — a bloodline carried too
far.

26

"THINKS THE CHECKOUT girl at Foodfair won't know what crap
he's buying if he turns everything upside down."

"Eats supper off newspapers on the floor."

"Puts that stuff into his voice to make him sound sadder."

He wrote such sooty truths about me in an otherwise hapless diary, but the penmanship of the pampered – such cusps, such struggly descenders! – was always hell on the eyes.

27

HE WAS SMOKING opinionatedly now, subsisting on seltzers and bars of absolute chocolate.

The bones he kept picking with me were skeletal of something bigger I should have been beginning to picture.

Then we were both reading the same book, but on different shifts. This was a levelling thing, a true story of a man's ruin, boosted from the hospital's lending library of no-joke literature of self-rescue. He read for pith alone, but carried the book into the bathroom with him. Brought it to our breakfast corner. Had it slammed open before him in bed while drawing things out from between his teeth or disporting a razor a final time for the day. The book accepted his shavings and flakes. They settled frankly into the narration. He kept at it until the book was auto-biographically crudded, a sampler of his cells and immoderate bodywide mire.

28

IT'S NOT THAT I didn't weigh on him, but I was hauled around in his mind without any of the swaddling my life and my living of it required.

Then it was heavy-skied autumn already. I had him cheating on me with my blessing.

I sent him off to whatever was eddying in other high-fore-headed men – scholarly lavatorians, killjoy attendants of fitting rooms.

There was one who divided the world into "have-nots and half-wits," and another whose money had pieces of other money paper-clipped to it, and their ilk was always more likable than mine, because I am of the kind that picks the wrong week to have finally had it with people.

My young man, though: I watched him pull from his tongue a hair displaying itself as a perfect, plucky ampersand.

29

LIVING, you see a lot of yourself, and what I saw was a man of straightforward hair, teeth reclusive in the teetering smile, one hand trysting with the other underneath any table or desk.

I wore ventilative shoes and took my foods at room temperature and wanted more out of people.

To hear me tell it, I had been one person, then condensed into somebody else, somebody more idiotical of our times.

30

OR YOU would have seen him, often as not, sitting alone on the low retaining wall outside a tourist center or at the foot of some moot monument or other. You would have fallen all over yourself for having been just the one to notice so utmost a loneliness in so baseless and unvisited a city. You would soon be flattering yourself that nowhere in his life was there so much as a co-worker who knew him to say hello to. Then a cloud or two would beg off overhead, or a blown leaf would blow right at you, because there was maybe a lake breeze from the brute lake that was farther off beyond the palings and bulkheads and embankments and the like. You would look his way again. He would not have moved so much as an atom. But you would see your mistake. For you would be in the grip now of the conviction that people, one person in rivalry with one or more repining others, were just that very instant waiting for him in other fractions of the city, having waited for hours, likely as not, and hating him for it, and hating themselves now, and ready to sever ties once and for all, if ties were what these stringily strung things, already shredded, must be suffered as terminology here.

You would have been right at least about me.

The others, had I gathered accurately, were the part owner of a concession-equipment-rental service and some molely someone with a mustache that looked mostly munched away.

31

OR I PICTURED myself three, four months ahead, being advised to "move on." But you could enter into people only so far and then had to come out the same way. There was never a way clear through. You were always back to where you started.

32

HE KEPT PACKING his things until they were parcelly and hard to make out under the twined rucklings of butcher paper.

Then they formed a lamentable plenty on the backseat of my sedan, driven finally through pinchy sunlight to the post office, where the clerk said, "These are going how?"

It was a reluctant city, this home of mine—a center of population but otherwise not at all solid to the local eye. No sooner did you leave the memorials downtown than the streets went uncertain.

Then the highway to the airport, four unlively lanes, and the airport, a torn-up one. Parked, went through the entrance sheds, let the moving walkway retard our progress. Then the terminal. He wanted the popular coffee. We read the program of departures. We kissed quickly and shrinkingly, in the manner of foreigners.

He left me leaving him.

FINGERACHE

HAVE YOU ever known me to be anything other than a woman shitty years of age but still standing by as much as I had lived of it, listening to her air the last of her intelligence on the family dirt, letting her butter me up for once the way she should have always? Because the day after the funeral it was her husband coming down to my level and wanting me to tell him whether he was saying it right—that since I knew where the things were kept and was up on the kids' chance triumphs at the chalkboard and their sizes in whatnot, wasn't I the one to have a go in what was left unstained of her clothes? (There was a cap-sleeved dress I could try on in the bathroom already.) But give him credit, I guess, for being the kind of man who kept his body set back a little from how he would have otherwise come across. It took effort to pick out just how off-base the hair was or to get an influential view of the minnowy mustache or, lower yet, a violet vein close to gaining the surface of his upper arm. I must have turned to him anew, this time with a more mature, closing eye.

Look: it's hardly as if I hadn't already put myself through marriages all my own—marriages small, it's true, of their kind. Which is to say it's a shit list I could be giving you now, a fecal census of bodies that were little more than backdrops for sickling emotions, though it was the emotions I remembered afterward, not the shapes of the men or anything else physically exclusive to them. I will bring up only the one I keep throwing in my face: he was a man of knowledge, granted, but before long he had slaughtered most of what he knew, or he had been losing acquaintance with it all along, or else the whole of it had swung suddenly away from him something awful—whatever the case, he had to go back and look everything up again by hand. We polished our differences in a house he bought from his parents for a dollar. I stayed only long enough to be accused of hiding out in a "personality."

So yes: I'm all for assuming novel difficulty in even moodier rearrangements of one on one. This latest husband made okay money, at least, but it was money with pieces, whole corners of it, gone. The house was mostly beaverboard and ungroomed carpet and concerted backdate appliances. I looked pushily at the walls and took his mind off things in the high heat of those first few weeks. There was innuendo even in how he rinsed out a glass, then set it, mouth downward, on the drainboard. I followed him into a bed that was on casters, brought to it some haphazard adult behaviors of my own. A low-lying smell was as much as he got out of me at first. Nights were fringed with the few things he said—"Far be it from me," "Not a day goes by."

One by one the children sought me out with pissy sorrows. The oldest said it would help if she knew who it was she was growing up for, and I said in that case, then, a way would have to be cleared for such a person. For a few days she started picking up after herself and was a little more wide-going in her affections. (A run of goodwill sometimes ran through her partway.) The middle child usually let a silence mature around her but now and again complained of shooting pains, of fingeraches and daintier misfunctions. These I told her to take as signs that her body had an interest in her and was making definite plans. (She prided herself on bringing back whatever might have rolled far beneath the furniture—her arms, her hands, were that meager already.) The youngest, a boy, was a little loose and unfortified in what he knew. He called the floor "the ground" and did not so much walk as trifle his legs forward: there were negligences, even criticisms of the filled world, in his lawless progress toward the table where supper could no longer wait.

One day, after lunch, I convened a fatherless full-house family assembly on pillows fronting the headboard of the master bed. There was copper trinketry, hobbied, untinkling, abroad on all three of the children—wristwirings, neck-hangings, anklets. None of what followed was to go beyond the room. I told them that should they ever be called upon to give the names of the parts of anything or another, it was always safe to go first with "base" and "projecture." I made it plain that I was a done-with portion of woman in the main but had once slapped along for years with arms the color of oysters. I explained that people made destinations of one another but no longer knew whom to live with; that people did not change but the spaces between them were forever going to have to. I said that as soon as they felt ready I would show them how to take any emotion and put a nice, bright costume over it. I said that you were always wrong about how it all goes wrong, because there were fewer people to put in place of the ones you had already gone aground in, and there was a shortage of places left to go on the people coming up next, but with the extra lips set out on her, a woman was never not saying something somewhere, and most of what got said was only that once you get to where your body feels hoaxed over you, you start to skip mirrors completely and just nerve your way direct to whoever else is got up as a woman or a man, and you get a good look from your eyepits at whoever it is until you're rewarded with the fate of finding your own features tugged and quirked just a little differingly onto the other's face—you're that far at large in people, a dead ringer for everyone else.

"She's saying there's no need to tell people apart?" the middle one said.

A night or two later, the man brought to our room something unsturdy and uncustomary in his face. He produced from his

pants pocket a smart little packet that I at first took for the color-
some wrappage of a prophylactic, but no, when he undid the
thing, I could see it was just a moist towelette. He squared it out
to full size, patted it first against his cheeks, gave a fast shine to
his forehead, the incline of his nose, the neck, then ran it up one
forearm and down the other; and then, seeing my hand opened
receptacularly, he balled the wilted thing and tossed it beyond
me.

"What could be that bad?" was as conclusive a lie as I could
provide.

They took me back, though, at a place where I had worked
once before. There were only so many reasons for a person to be
in the line of work I was in, and I had thrown myself open to all
of them at one time or another. I am not denying that I found
bloodshot relief in sitting at the desk again and having my lower
half neatly concealed from the remainder, but my arms were forever front and center. I suffered an insinking overintimacy with
the things. I would look down at the desk pad and find the arms
already there: there was no way around them. I started going out
of my way to convince myself that the arms were no more than
delegates of a commanding intelligence and not the intelligence
itself. But there they were again, ahead of me on the papers; I was
trailing behind. For a while I went in for longer, broader sleeves.
Then I started taking things out on the arms themselves. Bought
a watch with a wide strap that did away for good with an inch
and a half of the left one. Arranged a formation of bandages to
the left of the strap. Excited a patch of the right forearm with an
ink eraser until I had provoked a brush burn of sorts. Slickened
that with a discoloring preparation. Teased the little hairs off
both arms until the skin went red. I made as many examples of
them as I could slowly manage. When you're doing yourself out
of a life, I guess, the arms are always the last to go.

UNCLE

S HE WAS a milk-warm girl in bad odor with herself, glad to
have at last come down in the world. So she undoubled herself
from the boyfriends, the girlfriends, to better herself under my
roof. Mornings, she would struggle to the kitchen faucet and put
a finger to the underside of the spout. There was usually enough
water still hanging from it for the finger to come away with a big,
rudimentary drop. This she would use to loosen the crumbles of
sleep from the corners of her eyes. Breakfast was just soda she
stirred bubbleless with a paper straw.

I was the one stuck making the bed. I would interrupt myself
only long enough to raise a fingertip of her silverous lipstick from
the tube, then with rushed reverse turnings send it down again.

Afternoons, the sky volunteered its birds and its sun-showers.
We would be out on the patio again, each with a rubble of white
chocolate in a ruffled paper baking cup. The one skymark was a
radio tower, laddery and ablink.

Anything, she kept demanding, is the seat of a passion.

I would have to remind her, counteringly, that you don't pick
the person who fronts your life—you *get* picked, you watch the
picker's ankles vanish into the scrunched socks afterward (his
whole body going blank behind the blue-black of the uniform),

and the picker goes off in the starkest of transportations: you keep an ear cocked ever after for the return of his van and its paraphernalian clatter in the gravelled driveway.

You might consider chumming away at somebody your own age, she would say. Or who's hailing now from whom?

I would answer that we come by our austere perversions and then do our best to get out from under ourselves.

She wore her T-shirts in wearied, vanishing colors and would hold my hand retardedly in public. A short-streeted city was a habitual drive away. We would arrive just in time for the waning daytime plenty along the one horizonal avenue. We would walk around the people. The local public! They all had the look of having been made too much of already—each citizen a subsided mystery with hard feelings and staying power.

Afterward, restored to the house, close-piled on veers of the sectional sofa, we would haze each other into a shared, mutual nap. Her lips allotted little to mine, but there were always fresh runs of emotion inside.

Her heart never once cracked down.

EMINENCE

THERE WAS A TIME I would not hear of women, and a time I looked to them as my betters, and months when my heart went out to anyone done up as a person, but it was usually men I suited: men who liked to keep their words a little stepped back from their meanings and mostly wanted to know whether I was still in school or was hard on shoes. I would awaken to the poundings of one or another of them taking his elbowing ease in the shower stall. The bedside table would of course hold quarters, and a lone dime, out-of-date and valued-looking, and no doubt a patched-up, gadabout ten-dollar bill—I guess the test was simply how much I would be just the sort of boy to take. So I would let pocket change of my own drop to the floor in what I counted on amounting to an answering reproof, then top it with a spruce twenty. I would usually think better, though, and pick everything up, his and mine together, and disappear into my clothes and be gone before he was dry. Still, I suspect that I went unrepresented in much of what I ever did, if I get my drift even now.

There was a father, for instance, who wanted me to help save his daughter from him, or else he wanted to be saved from her— at some point I gave up keeping track of the ones I had been a party to seeing spared. There was a drumble of TV noise from the apartment below; that much is still with me. And he ticked off the points of nervy resemblance: upraised veinage, stand-out nose, teeth looking stabbed into the gums, arms unfavorable for even the joke sports. A broth of sweat came off him, and I hate it when they talk right into your mouth, but he kept it up until he convinced himself there was nothing set out between my legs other than whichever mishmash he figured on being a lot like hers. (At the time of which I write, circa my youth, there still were glories to be brought out in people behind their backs.) Weeks later I was introduced to the girl at some function I showed for. She was clean-lined, nothing new or unearthly—a desponding thing in a shirtdress, looking care-given and sided with beyond her years. The father was at the steam table, turning over the local foods. He had a tousled smile. "It's like you never left," he said.

I had been staying with four or five others on the top floor of a three-story sublet. Freaks of drapery to keep us from the morning sun, double-strength cosmetics and pills of the moment in handbags nailed shoulder-high to the wall—it hardly helped that this was in one of those little cities that had been thrown down at the approaches to a much bigger one once enough people were pinched for time or too moody for a commute. The town had already run afoul of its original intent, and there was a mis-given majesty to the newer, upstrewn architecture that left people flimsier in their citizenship, less likely to put their foot down. So we walked ourselves into recognizability in and around the plazas, the pocket parks, the foremost shrubberied square. You could run your feelings over one person and get them to come out on somebody else a little distance off. There was no need to even come face to face to be stuck in a failing familiarity forever.

People eventually answered any purpose or were no skin off my nose.

There was Joeie: clean-tasting but a trace too saline. Colored easily, needed his full eight hours every night, believed in taking each of his meals in public. His loves were drugstore luxuries and the fitting instant you knew for sure that something was finally finding its way down the wrong pipe. But sometimes the rope I woke up with around my ankles and wrists was only laundry line, and the knots were not even that serious.

And Tarn: he was either off doing somebody a wonder or having something further burned away from his complexion – you looked for the underlying advisory in his motions and let the whole of it loll in your understanding for a while. Nights I found the key to his car, there was a minor toll bridge I could have just as soon avoided, but I liked surrendering the warmed quarters to the collection attendant in the booth, his arm a sudden, perfected thing of the open air.

It was the night Tarn was first threatening to move out that an ex of his came across with a car trunk's worth of guitars. These were junk guitars, folksinger styles, with the strings raised penalizingly high above the fretboard. He wasn't satisfied until one was strapped onto me and he had his hand spread over mine to depress my fingers and get a few clunked chords going steadily. When he started to sing, the better part of the lyrics reminded you that with a stepmother and a stepsister, the prefixes alone, if you bothered to do even any of the thinking, made it all but expected of you to walk all over these women and, if you were still up to it, climb them stairwise to a height from which their originals might at least look easier to buy for, easier to mistake for two good eggs. It's not that I mind it when a pack of lies with real effort behind it gets pitched way over my head to somebody reliably cruel at a remove. But the song was going on and on, with too much chorus between verses. He later offered to make it up to us by driving everybody to a party in the city. There was a kid there with an isolative refreshment, something he alone had been given to eat. His fingers kept bringing it up from a plastic sandwich bag opaque with condensation. I was among the least encouraged to get an arm lilting leanly toward him. One or another of us stayed in touch with him for months afterward in notes that amounted to mostly "More soon."

I do not want to make it seem as if this is all we ever did. There was a neighbor lady's dog we agreed to feed when employments led her away. He was one of those full-natured, kerchiefed dogs that liked being bossed around. Days it fell to me to fill the dish, I did not so much call his name as thin it out to the scanty inner vowels, but the dog would still put in a complete, hustled appearance. I would watch him eat, take advantage of his company, draw myself out about things, any part of life I no longer was any part of, just to get listened to without bias or retention. There were also some weak-willed plants to be doused if I thought of it, and dresses that were all too tight on me and seemed to smell of more than just one person.

As for women overall, though, I went along with what Lorn had said about how they were set deeper within themselves and moved about reproductively in a world spaciously different from ours but sharing the same sorry places to meet up for a bite. And there was nothing to be held against any of them, either singly or in the dissatisfied aggregate, even if you now and then had somebody's sister coming forward with rundown makeup and a mugginess to her arms to tell you that the only reason you were a waiter instead of a grill man was so you could stand above people in seated couples and make a living looking down your nose. (There were only so many things you could say in return that would come across as both the truth and a dig. I had worked up enough of them to put into conservant, fallback rotation, but lately I just pointed to my groin and explained that if we give them names, it's because they spring from us, we bring them up, we're forever wiping their snotty little mouths.)

So what's left? The only other question still worth entertaining should not have to keep being only "Who else?"

Which I take to mean that the answer can't be parents, or even brothers and sisters, because we all were done with practically the exact same ones. Mother would signal the end of the conversation by saying she could feel inside her skull the precise contours of the space a headache would require, though she did not yet have the actual headache. Father had grown a beard that was more like a black cloud loitering in front of his face. (The beard was purposely mostly air.) The sister or brother was younger and had to have it drilled again and again into the head that it was one house if you came into it from the back and a different one altogether if you came in from the front: the people were the same, they were nice to you to your face, but nobody was being fooled: no one was living here everlastingly.

So that leaves whom else? Kittrick? Reese? Malin?

Or is this the one time the question becomes only "What other bones do you have in your body?" or "Where are you going to go with all those clothes?"

Because the answer could then be nothing more personal than that at the rebounding municipal college I was a figure of considerable scholastic mystique because I looked over my notes before the quiz and tried not to seem cross when the chairs had to be pushed back into a circle. The late-afternoon section of the summer course in speech was mostly boys, because it was mostly boys—repeaters, sweet-naturedly tardy, rug-burned in their undershirts—who had trouble sticking to their points and making it even as far as the middle minute of the three-minute impromptu. But when my turn came, I was slower-hearted in walking them all through how I saw it: that I was not the good listener everyone kept insisting I was, but I liked hearing people out the way I expected balloons to be quick about losing their air—I wanted the breathy, informative smell on their mouths right afterward; that the busy signal doesn't always have to sound like bleedbleedbleedbleedbleed; and that I could kick myself every time it did not come out to even so much as a syllogism no matter how often I got it stacked up onto the three needful tiers:

Major premise: You go with whatever is most available on people.

Minor premise: On men it is an eminence that luckily never lasts.

Conclusion: Except there was a farmers' market open only a couple of nights a week, and I could pick out the one to follow from a produce stand and into the men's room. There was just the one stall, and the latch was broken; it was up to me to lean against the door to keep up the privacy. Then the unzipping, and we were standing a polite foot apart, my arms retired now behind my back, his eyes already more wishless than mine. We let the things shy off from ourselves, boggle out the way they always did, twitch and dodge and stickle a little, until they were kissing unassisted. It was out of our hands, or none of our doing, and I could afterward witness the differences from me amassing in him almost instantly.

SPILLS

THE YOUNGEST of the girls had proposed herself out of the least promising of bodies and had ever after let her life take its line from the coercive slants and downturns of her sisters. She could go through their wastebaskets and find, hived away in envelope after envelope, discarded wafers of soap that were tongue-shaped from gloried use. These she could press against her oiling forehead until they stuck.

It was a town in which a night sky showed through the streets and trouble was often missing from things. To be fair, the only boys were sulkless local pollutables. Whichever one of them picked up the phone when she called would right away reach for anything close by to eat—suddenly unforgotten breakings from a pretzel, if need be, or jellied candies of abrupt magnitude. She would listen to the boys' encompassing swallows and take further swift steps against herself.

She became a forthputting girl of mixed intent.

Beyond the sweep of low-peaking buildings lived a boy about her age who had been held back one too many grades. With a slip of her heart, the girl would tug at the sails of the shirt that had been tucked too constrainingly into the boy's waistband. "Blouse it," she would say, and her hands went to work. She folded a cuff onto each of the red socklets the boy had been made to wear with the loose, flared shorts. His saliva was easy enough to elicit, and in it she could at least enjoy a loneliness to her taste, briny and warm, conclusional. She would pass the boy's stubbed, unfirm fingers inside her as far as they could be made to go.

Breadthless days piled everyone closer to the fall. The girl turned old enough to work, but the employee entrance was sticky and hard to get through with her handbag and magazine and snack. Her boss was a downtaken, suitorly man married full well. She returned home every evening to the expectable little pool of lucid soup that had been set out for her at the table.

She would let things faze her one at a time.

She would settle alertly for things.

The fingery disposition of bananas in a basket.

The way the high-set window cropped the crown of a tree.

The cuticular bloodiness to her hands; vague shinings in the nails.

Some nights she would come home to find a money order from her father, or another of the letters full of smart-mouthed affections, bruising tributes. He wrote of "rural torments," of "tumbles taken out of court," but would be "returning anon to resume certain backhanded familiarities under the mackerel skies of our town."

One afternoon her boss was fresh from a haircut. Slashes of gloomful hair still stuck to his forehead, were visible down his neck. He was all revolt and filthied principle. He had a bone to pick with everything she did—e.g., the ruthless, valedictory business she apparently resorted to with her hands after she shut the lowermost drawer of her desk.

The rest of this just parallels anything else entirely.

Viz., she trailed him to his car and became the woman I should have been instead—quick to disappear from as much as she understood of one person, quicker to get going in whatever might be likelier of the next.

I WAS IN KILTER WITH HIM A LITTLE

I ONCE HAD A HUSBAND, an unsoaring, incompact man of forty, but I often felt carried away from the marriage. I was no childbearer, and he was largely a passerby, minutely berserk in his bearing. We had just moved to one of the little cities that had been set out at intervals – they formed a kind of loose oblong, I imagine – in the upper tier of our state.

He had an unconsoling side, this husband, and a mean streak, and a pain that gadded about in his mouth, his jaw, and there was a bumble of blond hair all over him, and he couldn't count on sleep, on dreams, to get a done day butchered improvingly.

He drove a mutt of a car and was the lone typewriter mechanic left in the territory, a servicer of devastated platens, a releaser of stuck keys.

I would let him go broadly and unwitnessed into his day.

These cities each had a few grueling boulevards that urged themselves outbound. Buses passed from one city to the next and were kept conspicuously to their schedules, and I soon took to the buses, was taken with them: I would feel polite and brittle in my seat as a city was approached, neatened itself into streets and squares, then petered out again into bare topography. It never made much difference in which city I got off. I always had some business somewhere of a vaguely gracious, vaguely metropolitan sort, if only a matter of inquiring at a bank about exchanging some uncomely ones for a five. Sometimes I resorted to department stores, touched handbags, clutches (I have always preferred the undoing of any clasp); and I liked to favor a ladies' room with my solitude. I knew how to make an end of an afternoon, until the day lost pace and went choppy with a fineness I could refine the finality of.

It was mostly younger women on the buses – women barely clear of girlhood, dressed for functioning public loneliness in tarplike weighted cottons.

I one day sat down beside one.

My fingers were soon in the pan of her palm.

THIS CITY was a recent thing built in pious, cutback mimicry of someplace else. The streets were named after other streets.

I had been hired, probationally, as a substitute teacher, which meant I was not hated by any one student for any length of time, but I made enemies aplenty in the short haul.

I would write my name on the board, and then I would usually have one girl, a roupy-voiced thing, who would say, "Wait, I know you," and I would say, "I don't think so," and she would say, "Not from here."

Back in the practicums I had been taught to ask, "Who belongs to this paper?" Because you do run across cases where the possessory currents seem to be running more forcibly from the paper to the kid than the other way around. You're taught to feel something for anybody caught in that kind of pull, though I never once felt it.

I had, I hope, a dry, precise smile, a good-bye smile.

MY HUSBAND: he had sized his life to deprive it of most of the right things.

I had been meaning to get something in here of our incensed domestic civility, and the queered quiet of our nights, and the preenings of the weather all the following summer, a summer that never cut either of us in on its havoc and seethe, but the mind's eye is the least reliable of the sightholes, and I might have been looking all along through only one of those.

It was availed away, our marriage.

We got tardier about every fresh start.

IF I AM TALKING them up again, these women brimming hectically now on buses, it can't be only to keep throwing pinched perspectives over their low points, every rut in their loveliness.

It's just that I tend to get all devotionate when I sense sore spots and unaired ires in any shrewd mess densening suddenly in my ken.

A Tuesday, for undiscouraged instance: a vexable, vapory girl.

My one hand mulling its way into a pocket of her coat.

(To join hers there at last.)

My other hand fluffing up the leg of her pants.

(The hair on her shin a chestnut-brown emphasis.)

I helped myself to their charity.

RUTHFULLY OPEN ARMS, blind sides, always a general alcoholature to their breath—it was true a few of them might have been cautioning me all along to look out for myself, but I took that to mean what? That I was the fittest object of my own suspicions?

Women of muddled impulse, lonely beyond their means—I let my drowsy heart drowse around.

THEN IT WAS DECIDED it was time to fix on just one of them. I was on a bus homeward from work. She was steadfast of face, and it was a situated face, or my idea of one, but her dress screened her off so completely that the breasts were cryptic, the legs undefined.

Ideally, the way we sat, the way our forearms were set out in a line, her bracelet should have slid with ease from her wrist to mine. But the rumps of our hands were too thick to permit a crossing.

Then her apartment, a barracksy large, lone room: tenants on either side of us, and above, beneath, making overheard but unintelligible dead-set headway.

She had sweepy arms, a squall of dark hair, eyes a slubby brown. She spoke through prim, petite teeth of favors she was owed.

There was relief in how quick we could find the hardness in each other.

THEN WEEKS, scrapes of inquisitive affection, kisses kept quiet and dry, unluminary movements not undear to me, a clean breast made here or there, every passing thought treated to a going explanation (people combine unneatly), an inaccurate accusation, a principal I had to have it out with.

They weren't hours, these classes; they weren't even forty-five minutes—they were "periods," which sounded to me as if they were each at once a little era and the end you had to see decisively put to it.

I would be summoned from school to school, grade to grade, and I would advance through a class, a subject, a unit, by picking on yet another nobody undergoing youth, and I would peer into her worried homeliness, let a trait or feature advocate itself for half an hour's discrediting endearment.

Eyes, maybe; eyes of a sticky green that looked fuddled with the world and its ongoing insistence that things, people, remain detailed and unalike.

Or an unblunt arm unsleeved in late autumn and within esteeming reach, though I had come to believe miserably in seeing arms not as the pathway to a person but as the route the body took to get as far afield of itself as it could.

Evidence pointed directly to other evidence, never directly to me. What influence did I have? I spoke from notes.

WHEN YOU ARE no good at what you do, it does you no good to triumph at whatever you might come home to, either. My husband was in fact my second one. I should be making a case for the first, for the avenues of feeling I must have taken with him, though he mostly just roved from room to room between charley horses, was studious in his insults, twidged a slowpoke finger into where I still trickled against my will.

Let me remember him, at least, for being the one to teach me that there was only one polite way left to say "yes," and that was "I'm afraid so."

I AM ADMITTEDLY leaving out a kid I left eventually with an aunt, my one uncornering aunt, but I imagine I did later write a letter to be given to the kid when the kid finally aged overnight.

I wrote it in emotional accelerations of my pen on hotel stationery on an evening the fitness of the word *evening* struck me for once, for isn't it the business of that first reach of the night to even out any remaining serrations of the day?

I was a woman heaping all alone into her thirties.

Things allowed me mostly lowered me.

MY YOUNG WOMAN, then: she was technically out of the nest, but there was a parent she reported to, and I must have known there were other goads.

In the night-light, I could see where she had been C-sectioned. A weak grief usually strutted her up. She sometimes thumbed an hour aside with habits, practices; brought an abruptly feared finger down on the pricket of a candleholder, maybe, to gloat over dribbleting blood. But the nail of the finger had been cheered an opera pink, or a mallow purple, and there was nothing uncourtly in her intonations.

I was thus kept milling in her feelings still.

For a living, she banged about tables in a downstairs restaurant scaled back now to only breakfast and a rushed late lunch. She would settle her stomach with formally forked portions of what had unsettled it in the first place.

But how best to be usefully afraid for her? I could never get a sense of where others might be perched in her affections.

Her name—I dare not draw it out here—was a huddle of scrunty consonants and a solitary vowel, short. I should have done a better job of learning how to say the thing without its getting sogged somehow.

A FAMILY? That was where you got crooked out of childhood.

I had been sixteen when I grew into my mother's size—an already tight and terrible ten. Our wardrobes overlapped for a while, then no longer got sorted at all. We would pick a day's dark attire out of the dryer, and had to go from there.

Or you could go back even further, to when you are barely untucked from childhood and finally get the full run of your body, and feel secure in all its workings, then learn that everything on it will now have to be put to dirtier purpose.

But my brother? I was in kilter with him a little.

I turned on him, then turned back.

There was already wide plight to my tapering life.

ONE NIGHT, though, I had to use her bathroom. It was mostly men's things in there—shaving utilities, drab soaps, an uncapped deodorant stick with a military stink to it.

When I came out, the phone rang.

"Let it sleep," she said.

(The handset had, after all, a "cradle.")

Then later, someone slapping away at the door.

The slaps were all accumulating at one altitude at first, but then travelled unmightily down the door panel to the knob.

Then sudden, fretful turnings of the knob.

We listened, hands united, until the commotion at the door was a gone-by sound, followed by the gone-by sounds of feet in the hallway, then of a car entered, roused, driven expressively away.

PRESCRIPTION OBLIVIALS gave her an assist with her moods, veered her toward a slow-spoken sociability sometimes, sometimes made her meaner.

We would sit down dearly to a dinner of whiskery import vegetables, close-cropped meat gone meek in the sauce, everything on side plates, everything a lurid obscurer of itself.

But why lie when the truth is that the truth jumps out at you anyway?

Before me, so she claimed, it had been a narrow-faced shop-maiden with a muggy bosom and a catastrophal slant to her mind.

To hear her tell it, there were girl friends (two words), there were girlfriends (one word), there were friend girls, and there were women. Women were never your friend.

BABY TALK like that must have put the lacquer back onto my life for a while.

I stood up quite handsomely now to my husband's entire, perspirant heights.

One morning I thumbed out most of the teeth from a comb of his, stuck them upright in rough tufts of our carpet—whatever it then took to get a barefoot person hurt revolutionarily.

BUT THE DAYS arched over us and kept us typical to our era. It was an era of untidying succors, follied overhauls.

Her manager gave her more hours.

Her feelings came down to me now in just dwindlements of the original.

She started showing up in the snap judgments of a glass-blowing uncle, and was an aunt herself to two nieces already girthed and contrarious.

We had them over, those two, to her place, our table. They had been lured through youth with holiday slugs of liquor, had put themselves through phases but always stopped short of complete metamorphosis.

The younger was the more bridelike. Skewy eyes, a dump of dulled hair. A sparge of moles on the neck, the shoulder.

The older's shoe kept knocking against my own.

She picked a hole in her biscuit, didn't seem to have any tides dragging at her.

They each later took me aside to tell me what they had had the nerve to collect, study, and forsake. Thick books read to detriment; tiny, frittery animals – need I say?

Afterward, the woman and I alone, the night gone quickly un-infinite: I kept seizing things – household motes and the like – out of the broad, midbody bosh of her hair.

But if I say I felt something for her, would that make it sound as if I felt things in her stead, bypassing her completely?

Because that might too be true.

WHEN YOU'RE A RENTER, a tenant, an apartment-house impermanent, you make do without cellarways, attics, crawl spaces: there's little volume your life can fill.

So you take it outside to the open air – into thin air, you've already corrected yourself.

The eye doctor started calling my husband a "glaucoma suspect." There were drops and a dropper on the nightstand, pamphlets of attenuated portent.

I got better at tugging away the context from around every least thing. Something as unchaotical, I mean, as the compact she had suddenly stopped caring for. It no longer made the daily dainty descent into her purse.

I got alone with it, unclamped the clamshell casing.

Spoofed much too much of the powder onto my nose, my cheeks.

Waited.

Waited even longer.

No alarms to report then and there, of course, but I must have ever after felt eaten away a little more around the clock.

MY WEEKS with this bare woman dipped deficiently toward winter. She either worried herself back into my attentions, or a day got minced into minutes we just wished away. Her love for me, in short, was a lopsided compliment, longer in the rebuke than in the glorifying.

The freshest snow on the streets already grooved and slutted by traffic.

ANOTHER NIGHT of roundabout apologizing, and she reached for a shoulder bag, not one of her regular daytime totes. She tipped it all out, fingered everything preservingly where it fell.

The whole business was already looking a little too votive to me.

First the smoot, the flaked razures and other collects, she had abstracted from the gutter between blades of an overemployed disposable shaver. (It had taken, she said, the corner of an index card to reclaim it.)

Then, in a mouth-rinse bottle, a few fluidal ounces of sea-blue slosh from a compress that had been used whenever there were immaculate agonies behind a knee.

And a smutched inch or so of adhesive tape from a homemade bandage, into which pores had confided their oily fluences. All stickage had long gone out of the thing. (She dangled it inexactly across her wrist.)

It had all been her sister's, she said, if a sister is who it had been.

I am always in doubt of whoever can't die right away.

SHE WAS GONE some nights, too. Things happen when you are younger and have it in you to pinpoint your satisfactions.

I would take the bus to look in on my husband. In my absence, life had scarcely scratched at the man. He never bothered going through my pockets or sought secrets in my miscellaneals. His point of view was exactly that—a speck, something too tiny to even flick away. We were in the bathroom; he was razoring the daily durations of hair from his cheeks, his chin. I was sitting shiftily along the brim of the tub. There was the hankering hang of his thing. I let it fool itself out toward me.

DAYS WERE not so much finished as effaced. You caught sight of new, unroomy hours looming through the old. Then months more: months of fudging forward unfamished. Then a Sunday night, a worldly evening, finally.

We got off the bus, the woman and I, at the first town we came to. It was a paltry locality with a planetarium, a post office, a plaza. The plaza had a restaurant. We went in, ordered, raked through each other's romaine, thinned out the conversation, set off for the restroom together. Somebody had taped to the mirror a reminder that hands should be washed for thirty seconds—the exact length, the sign went on to say, of a chorus of "Happy Birthday." We thus sang as we soaped the other's dickering fingers, but when we came within syllables of the end of the third line, where you have to put in the name of the "dear" celebratee, we broke things off.

It was the same driver for the trip back—not a nice man.

This being my history, I snapped out of my marriage, pieced myself back into the population, prodded and faulted, saw red, then wed anew in wee ways.

This husband and I soon set a waning example of even our own business.

I later fell in with a girl who kept a cat on her head to stay warm.

I was mostly of a mood to pollute, and she was frank in her dreams, which she logged, but a liar in all other opportunities.

Then years had their say.

HER DEAR ONLY FATHER'S LONE WIFE'S SOLITUDINIZED, PEACELESS SON

IF, THEN AGAIN, I had been put on earth to hurry up and come between any noise the world might think it finally needs and whoever is fittest to produce it, who better to have been still living at home when it came time at last for hers? The day, I mean, when your best friend throws you over for an emissary from the opposing sex, and for a glorifiable afternoon your bellyaching strikes just the right note of retrenched intimacy and spite, but spite that is holding out some hope.

For we were brother and younger sister, cobelligerents on the centerpiece of a pushed-apart sectional sofa, and I told her, naturally, that when it had happened to me, the "friend" was a boy with a disadvantaging face, big and round, much of it still to be filled in, and before the day was out, I had gone sick for the first venereal do-gooder to come my way. He was a seller of house paint. He brushed the fingers of one hand down my arm, escorted me to a car, and, before I parted from him later, wanted to go over it with me one more time—the difference between *hiding power* and *coverage*, the former being the capacity of a paint to disguise that which is to be painted over, the latter merely the area at last thus treated, expressed in square inchage or however else it could still be stomached.

So I told my sister that I did not want the two of us to be wasting her day away, or holding her back from people, but she said no, there was no real rush just yet; and if, in putting her up for depiction here, I insist on having a few stippled liberties taken with the complexion, and the teeth kept completely under wraps, and the hair dinged and torn up afresh, and the sleeves drawn all the way down and buttoned beyond the wrists, the tack I am taking, please understand, is to preserve her this side of recognizability on the one hand and just shy of the very picture of forgottenness on the other. But what wooing good would it do me to keep her in anything other than the skirt that was just plain curtaining? Because sunlight had caught the line of her shinbone suchwise that the skin above it was aglow, and you don't let light like that just run off from a person, though you don't go crying it up too publicly, either. You might, at most, assure her that an hour spent in your company right now would hold its own against any hour she was likely to pass with anyone who had not come to such good-sport maturity under a common roof; and no sooner had my sister signalled shruggy agreement than she uprighted herself, set the lower leg swinging from the fulcrum of her knee, and the shining line that had got its start on her shin spirited itself out across the room to the telephone stand and let itself sink into the oaktag portfolio, the accordion-pleated clutch, that I toted about instead of a wallet.

So I got up from the sofa to claim the thing, and on the way back, having unsnapped the elastic band, then fishing around inside, bringing up a catch of fives and tens, I asked whether she had troubled to notice that people, loneful ones, had taken to writing in the margins of their currency – beseechments and pleas, mostly, to pass along – and since I am not a person who ordinarily requires a reply, I said only, "What ever shall we be writing on our very own?" I lowered myself beside her again and ventured a ten-dollar bill face-up and longwise onto the downy wealths of her leg, then inched a stick-pen between fingers of hers already spread acceptantly. There's an unpuncturing penmanship held in reserve, of course, for just such moments when there's pertinent skin – snug-pored, flushingly tender – underneath; and it was with just such leniency of longhand that she wrote, in the upper margin of the bill: "Hindsight is always 50/50!!!" I brought out a narrow-barrelled ballpoint for myself and, starting in the right margin, then working my way down and around, wrote: "I am grateful even for people whose beauty is just a sideline to how they really look." But her writing hand had already set out catchingly for the left margin before mine was entirely withdrawn.

Again: is it that one thing leads to another, or that the other has been tugging the first one forward all along? Because the instant your sister is whispering into your mouth, words lose all consonantal bounds.

They're down to just vocalic mist.

Ah-aw was as much as I could make out of it.

Back off?

Dad saw?

Paths cross.

THEN YEARS.

I saw my parents to their graves. (They went neck and neck in a November remembered mostly for the rectitude of its weather.) I moved to a close-by city with a dip in its population. (People were either accumulating attentions intended for others or picking over available holes.) There were days, though, when the dick was deputative of a clear thinker and got itself responsibly aloft: I thus married easily enough. I will shoot ahead of the peculiars of her rearing and emotionality, and report only that the woman and I prospered ammonially in close quarters, the washing machine was almost never not going, neither of us was ever got the better of in the heart-to-hearts, but I put myself out of her misery early.

I threw in with a man about my age who made a game of losing a finger in the hairy slough at the foundation of my spine. (I

could count on a separate, alkaline smell to him come morning.)
Then a woman who said I looked like someone who would be
good with tools. (She had lineature already around the mouth
and was unrepaired overall. But I liked taking orders for a while
and co-signed for the pleasant car she said her thoughtsick son
required.) Next the son himself, minus the mother and motion-
able only in the ebb and flow of semesters. (Nights, he sat up late
in a shower wrap and turned the heavyweight workbook pages.
The hand I now and again admitted between his legs came out
unclaimed and little different.)

So agreed: that allegiances, alliances, turned on a dime, and it
was a dime that stuck to whoever's bare back was turned to me
at the time, then worked itself loose and dropped to the floor so
I could stoop for it and put it later toward the newspaper, the
thinning local of good comfort, which ran the discount-chain
ads in which I had been following the downsloping progress
of an unmistakable pair of long-natured arms from sale to sale,
through one set of abbreviated sleeves and then out of another,
no matter that the face above got cropped and that the ink, meted
out in unevenness, had blotched everything before I ever got my
spattering chance.

I lived like this, yes, and took to calling everyone "Miss" for
the nice emphasis it put on my failure to have made any of them
even palely mine. My seniority at the office began developing tiny
pockets of fallibility, creases too easily taken for weals. I lacked the
criterional patina of my peers, or so it got sworn in a file somewhere. I alone was never invited to join in on even the wider-
blown windfalls. A "failure to thrive," in short—unless it was
some higher-up's mortuary newborn I kept overhearing them
describe. The afternoon I was told to empty my desk, I dropped
eventually to my knees to get the carpet smoothed underneath. I
teased the tufts into a uniform, satisfying, outbound drift.

But was it only "years" I said above? For it must have been decades I meant: a couple of them—solid and volumed and colum-
nar, though demolishable the moment someone thought to say,

"If you don't mind my asking," because the oncoming question was either "How goes your sister?" or "Your dentist die?" The former I could turn my back upon in time to remind myself that the error of my ways was actually an assorting of errors, though there was only the one way, which, once I came into a sense of it as nothing more than a *route*, did not even seem to pass through any of the places where actual dirt could have been done.

But on the matter of the teeth: I concede that there were breaks, crannies, in the bulwark of cracked enamel I held my tongue behind. (Who has time to be minding bony minutiae?) I figured one or two of them must have snapped off in the thicker and gristlier of the things I ate. (Meals were taken counterside, in stand-up haste and minimized light.) Others might have backed out while I slept, then got carried away, and drowned, in deep-some overnight salivas.

So if that is all this needs to be–a behindhand recountal of a man who may have let a thing or two slide–then it might as well come to a head one day not too many months after I had settled in with somebody new (a great one he was at first for paddling the air between us with hand mirrors, fanning me with gilt-framed glimpses of everything amiss between my lips), and I got myself dressed and went out for a comparisonal look at the run of teeth in other open mouths–the layouts and lineups, their bias and skew, how snugly everything was packed into the lavish salmon of the gums.

It was early afternoon: the people about were mostly older people. I came to a dental studio with a sign welcoming emergency walk-ins. Was admitted, told to lie back and relax in the chair. It was not a dentist but an assistant; I tasted beauty soap on the instruments. She had barely begun inspection before whispering, "Oh, you didn't want to hurt anybody–is that what it was? Because these are well above the fray: ground to a fault and altogether fine. A few may have dropped below the gumline, but not for long. In short, I find much to admire. I wouldn't change a thing."

I said, "Now the dentist has a look?" She did not treat it as a question that had an answer. I went out to the receptionist's station. "They're not talking to each other," the receptionist said. I paid; was handed a receipt and then, afterthoughtfully, a much-thumbed leaflet called *You Can Hardly Even Notice*. It was printed in one of those frail, sticklike typefaces that make everything look a little religious and overpersonal. I read it on my way out.

Courtesy permits a synopsis?

A man who claims to have lost his teeth to love is walking down the sidewalk when he notices an approaching figure still several blocks off. Not a moment to lose. He stoops for some flower-bed pebbles, orders them archwise into the gutter of his lower gums, vows for now to go without swallows. Reaches next for a piece of blown-about cardboard, beneficially off-white; tears off a strip twice the length of a finger; makes thirteen tiny, half-way tears at roughly quarter-inch intervals along the lower edge; tucks the strip only far enough under the canopy of his upper lip for a curved and dividered line to achieve jaunty visibility just beneath. The approacher by now is less than one block away. It's a woman, obviously. Saliva puddles in his mouth. He smiles sloshily as she walks past, arms aswing. But how much does she see? For the tract ends on the burdenful note that, unbeknown to the man, the woman's long sleeves are stuffed entirely with kneesocks and wadded homework papers, except for mouth-wash-bottle caps poking out where the elbows would ordinarily, jointedly, go; that the fingers of the glove sewn to the wrist of each sleeve are filled weightily with dampened sand; that the sandbox from which the sand was spooned belonged once to the woman's daughter, who, as a child, and still later, was a clinger, a clutcher, a tugger at the sleeve, a hand-puller, a wrist-wrencher, an arm-twister—a hanger-on, in short, who grew up to become the only person ever eligible to behold the amputatory triumph of her love.

Below the last sentence, though, the receptionist or someone else had written, reconsideringly: "There's a man in a shanty behind the old shopping center who's been doing some interesting things overnight in ceramic."

I went out there while I still had the verve to hear news I could take hard.

The door was open just a trifle. There was a worktable inside, and a washstand, and a man and a much younger woman sitting on patio chairs in front of a kiln. The man got up and moved toward me, reached into his mouth to lift out the lower crescent of his dentures, rinsed it at the washstand, then placed it in my one hand and a laminated snapshot in the other. It was a print taking in a little business district in a sunny aerial sweep; some of the buildings had been circled helpfully in red. I looked back and forth between the photograph and the shammed teeth long enough until I could let on with a nod that, yes, I had begun to make everything out – the mansard-roofed hotel memorialized, underexplicably, in the lower-left molars, and the across-town hospital in the lower right, and a limited line of commercial buildings in the lank rhomboids of the incisors, and the water tower in a plasterlike bicuspid pitched so steeply, I had to hope its upper-arch counterpart had been hollowed out to allow the man the boon, at least, of shutting his mouth without too much harm.

I set the things on the worktable, expressed admiration, then added that I thought I could probably get by with just a partial. Here the woman let out a quick little cry of affinity, and as she got up and came closer, I watched her uncatch some chainlets that were belted about zodiacally in the vault of her open mouth, fastened here and there to kernelly canines and some stumps toward the rear. She lined out four or five of the things, gleamingly, in the bowl of the man's palm: fanglements I would have anywhere else taken for overintricated fishing lures, maybe, or the contraptious miniature hardware you resorted to when nobody else's hands were steady enough to hang a picture treasured too long in secret – except there was a charm or token or two dazzled along the length of each.

The man assured me that I could go with tooth-colored ones if I wished ("You can't eat with them in, of course"), but either way I would be pleased to discover in my speech a fresh, enlivening meander. He told her to put them back in and favor us with talk. I watched the fingers hooking, reinstalling, and then, if I heard her right, she was saying, in a voice that sounded bitten away at from within: "This isn't kissing. It's just the way he goes about getting a better feel for how everything is spaced out inside." And in fact the man's tongue was already lukewarm and adart in my mouth.

Afterward, I told them there was somebody at home I would have to talk it over with first.

I AM CALLING him my familiar here, but in sorry truth he had begun unversing himself in me almost from the outset. It was an intimacy, after all, founded on little but joint dislikes and congruent cross-purposes. Not that I was his opposite—I was more like his reverse, going back on things he was just now coming into. But his face! He had a face that had you taking sides again every time. You were expected to either fall all over yourself the moment you caught sight of the hair he had hanging in a pair of black, glossy sheets, or else woo yourself half-blind with the weak green havoc of his eyes.

He was not yet a full-fledged tailor, mind you, but freelanced in alterations to trousers that gave the wearer more play in the seat and the crotch. Men in shirttails and underpants stood stockstill for him in a room with a separate, backstairs entrance. I went up there sometimes when he was out spreading word of mouth even wider. There were pants pegged to the walls in hangered fraternities, and a couple of full-length mirrors slanted to afford a plunging perspective, because what sort of man did not need to see himself relieved of his face and that much the deeper in things? My own body got its start an inch or so north of a belt orbiting loosely, unupholdingly, in the loops, and ran itself down to the dust-hoarding creases in the vamps of my shoes. That's

how I remember myself at my best, anyway – cropped at last to
the lower, better half.

I hope I am speaking for more than myself, then, if I insist
that when two men pool their solitudes, there is none of the
ruthless, finite symmetry still said to obtain between any woman soever and a man, but only an obstructive redundancy intent
on doubling itself out indefinitely. I offer as lonesome, sidewise
example the fact that after we chose the house, we could never
settle on a fixed purpose for any one room. You worked your
way down the hall and opened any door to yet another independent setting in which to eat or lie down or hide. These are not
criticisms or judgments but simply flat-out truths I have tapered
just enough for them to come eventually to the point that when
he brought people around at night, clients and prospects, men
of a mind to leave shallow, souring impresses of themselves on
somebody else's sofa for an hour, it would make little difference
in which room I was keeping to myself upstairs. There would be
spells of laughter, then a lone voice sending itself up through the
floorboards, then sudden, unanimous inquiries about the house
and whoever else might be acquaintable within. Sooner or later
I would hear myself come up for description as "an old family
friend getting back on his feet."

That night, I heard one of them take the stairs, treat himself
to a tour, then loiter at the doorway of the room in which I had
unwound myself for a nap on a much-trod gangway of a carpet
runner. He came in, lowered himself to a sociable crouch, and
explained, unencouraged, that when you worked for an outfit
that was mostly cheatery anyway and was down now to just the
two phones, you got confused about which one was ringing,
though it was usually hers, so if you had already, mistakefully,
reached for yours, you had to fall quick to mock-dialing, and you
understandably wanted nothing more to do with the woman
other than starting to dress a little like her, which meant only
absorbing her ruling colors and throwing them back at her a day
later in the downcourse of a scarf or the baggy vastness of a shirt-

front, not out of snot-nosed deference, because it would be lost
on her, but in the interest of whatever continuity that backbiting
best provided as you made passage from the delicately errorful
hours before lunch to the fouler hours of digestion thereafter.

By now I had been made curious enough by the man's voice,
which sounded as if something were cutting into it, or costing
him some crispness, that I lifted my head a little and turned his
way. The teeth in the upper half of his smile looked unstationary.
Not as a unit, though – these were teeth that seemed individually,
isolatedly, motional and asway. I tried to push my eyes along to
anything else, entertaining myself first with the campaign of gray
in his stubble, then with the wire-spun consequentials of his eye-
glass frames, and to be saying something I said that what's worse
is when the firm is pairing off every stick of polished deadwood
with a new hire behind just one door, and it's a door she covers
right away with kindly cartoons and screwball newspaper cut-
tings, and before long you are so worried about passersby walking away in a smiling conviction of some united, craven good
humor in force behind the door that you tape to it a little note
saying "All postings by – " and then see that her name gets a large-
lettered outspelling in marriage-hyphened, horse's-ass entirety.

But who doesn't know when it's only his mouth being talked
to, and whatever is most equivocal by way of teeth inside?

Because he reached between his lips, jerked the thing out,
draped it stickily and braceletwise across my wrist. It was just a
few slicings of board-game dice that had been filed down further,
then trained along the length of some black elastic with a tiny,
molar-encircling clasp at either end. He hitched the ends of it
together with a pitiless pinch, then started toward the stairs. But
I did not let him spoil it, the moment most to my liking: when
the house had gone quiet except for the drawn-out smack-smick
of the suckage that people expected we lived for but in fact was
just the way every other one of us, down at last on bended knee,
knew best to tender his pledge of farewell.

IF NOTHING ELSE, then, I caught a bus late the next morning to the outlying locality where I had been set upon by the faultful, godsend sister in the first place. I stepped off at the public library. At the reference desk I inquired after any picture of the town that might have been taken from on high. The woman hurried off in a sidesway, returned with a sesquicentennial panorama in a back number of the auto-club monthly. It was just hobbywork, irresolute in its focus, but I could stare down into the sprawllessness of the neighborhoods and make out the upward pleadings of individual roofs. I must have had a look on my face, because the woman was saying, "If it's that important." She had the scissor blades already parted.

On the bus back, my pen was wobbly, and I doubt I was circling the exact houses. (The photo, as I have said, fell short of splendor.) And I was confining myself to just fourteen—enough alone for the lowers. I would have the remaining ones out a.s.a.p., then let the ceramist behind the shopping center trick something up for me in terra cotta, scale a little of the town down into my bite, make it bear annihilatively on any further talk of time going faster when you're giving yourself away.

I numbered the circles as chronologically as I could.

The annotations were typed up later and are laid out for you hereinbelow, precisely as I dumped them all on him, because I am a believer in treating everyone equal, or at most as one and the same:

1. 63 EAST JUNIPER STREET

Since the living-room carpet was deep-tangled and untamed, she would fetch any fallen pencil by sliding a sheet of letter-writing paper, corner first, beneath it, then pick the pencil up off the *paper* —a civilizing enough thing to have been in her nature to learn from me while our parents still could sleep.

2. 87 EAST JUNIPER STREET

I taught her, of course, that although it was easy enough to get the sound cleansed from most of whatever she did (e.g., destining her pee, as she had already discovered, not into the water proper but onto a cloudpack of tissue allowed first to mount purposively in the bowl), things would be better for all concerned if, instead, she timed any little personal noise of hers to coincide with a larger, outer sound (postponing a cough, say, until the instant a cupboard door was clumsily shut, or bringing her whispers in unison with the rustle of pages being turned across the room in Father's evening paper). In next to no time I thus was hearing her, bodily, behind every household stirring and thud.

3. 292 NORTH MAIN STREET

Just the grade school from which she brought home papers of hers the teachers had not cared for. (Sheets dressed with disobeying, hideaway penmanship that lapped over itself from line to line. Or others on which you could make out words, but the words had all been chained together with hyphens, and the hyphens were darkful things, thick as equal signs.) I acted the patron, paying her in pennies she could take to the man who sold cough drops by the piece. Better for her to prefer anything coming cherrily to nothing on the tongue instead of whatever a teacher might still be working up to such expert verticals on the board.

4. 1031 WEST GROSVENOR STREET

We were always moving, but hardly moving far—a couple of blocks up the same sharp street, or only one street over, or three or four bountiful doors down. I wish I could say it was just the neighbors and their noises, or the animals the neighbors began favoring, or a bay window too beholden to its view. But it was more often a weakness, indiscernible earlier, in the scheming out of the rooms themselves, how perplexively one led off onto the next, so that you had to put yourself through this room, then that one, to reach a place to which you thought you were bearing an emotion still distinct and unopposed, though once you got there, it was scarcely any longer even yours alone to feel.

5. 211 NORTH EIGHTH STREET

I told her that between any two people in a family there was a big block of feeling for them to do with as they wished.

I spoke her mind.

I lowered her sights.

6. 835 NORTH EIGHTH STREET

The night I let it drop that the body is mostly a body of water, she tried to boot me out of her room but was prevented, I sensed, by a leg already fallen asleep.

7. 17 SOUTH FRONT STREET

We came by contrary motions to the same place—a paradise of vacant shade beside the moving van. I re-introduced myself, this time, as her dear only father's lone wife's solitudinized, peaceless son.

Shirtless in her dun-colory jumper.

The umbral hollows of her underarms.

A dry run for everything certain to follow.

8. 71 WEST RAILROAD STREET (REAR ALLEY)

I told her I was an only child but had consented to being repeated here and there in the sketchiness of her chin, in the forehead that was all uphill, in her fragrance without undersweat.

She was just a later arrayal of what had figured foremost on me.

I had a right to require all of it back.

9. 74 WEST WATER STREET

We were side by side in the laundry room the night the lightbulb finally burned out. There was the petite spectacularity of the filamentary ping, and then I let her be the first to do something, and then I did something in character with it, only much wider-about, in the interest of knowing better trouble.

10. 333 SOUTH EIGHTH STREET, APARTMENT 2-C

Days had the same onsweep, and off-bearings, and hours with me lost in earshot.

My mother telling my sister, "Because you have friends and he still doesn't."

My sister telling my father, "He says the rooms have us divided up all wrong."

11. 1414 EAST LOCUST STREET

When she went off for her bath, I donned her watch for any indrawing warmth still current in the strap, got as much of the clutch of her jewelry on me as I could manage, given that I was broader all around, and harder on things I wore out. (Only the tops of her dotty pajamas could fit me without stitches starting to split.)

12. 19 NORTH GRAVEL HILL ROAD

Or when you are the wrong way around in how you now feel, you can say: Here's the person herself, and here's the person scraped together on top. Then the way is cleaner to things.

13. 393 EAST LOCUST STREET

My assurances, again, that whatever she felt hanging over her head would appear to others as no more than skyward extenders of her hairdress – raylets, wingings.

14. 2187 BUENA VISTA DRIVE

I eventually let a boy in her grade play himself slimly into my hands. He had a deep, lax mouth stocked with teeth enough like hers in the cuspidal setbacks above and in the lusterless huddle below, and arms that in their blunt, bluff panels could have passed for the ones she tossed overboard in her naps, and eyes nicely competitive with hers in their downcast hazel exactions, and hair – unrationed on her head, kept almost portionless on his – of a resemblant, fellowly nutmeg-brown. We coaxed his parents into letting him exchange his room upstairs for some moist space in the basement. I steeped myself in his gamier hours before the first of them returned from work. There was the thutter of a dehumidifier to draw off any sound I got made on him. They should count for all the world as something of a heyday, then: the fingerworn weeks until he said, "I want to thank you for bringing me to the brink of girls."

IN CASE OF IN NO CASE

M Y YOUNGER BROTHER was having trouble with his dreams. The trouble was that some of them had been obviously, insultingly, intended for somebody else. They arrived in his sleep after having been turned away by other people. He would recount the story lines for me. We would have no luck finding any of his belongings anywhere inside. We would look and keep looking.

This was the brother who "tonsured" his arms and legs. "The well-groomed man," he insisted, "is never not shaving." It was up to me to hold the lighter whenever he did the bust-ups of his acne with the pin of a name badge he had to wear for work. His answering-machine presentation was a greetingless, trilled avouchment of his being out, gone, anywhere else. I would sometimes call just to take it in, all that tonal flaunt of progress, forgettery.

I saw some valiance in how he raked us over the coals.

Neither of us was allowed to bring men into the house.

My mother was fluent in all the current forms that violence took between mothers and their middle sons. Every day she re-befriended me. I would go crazy over whatever she heated up on the stove. She had her own way of deconcocting what had been cooked originally. We were big on off-flavors.

She would tiptoe to the room where my father endeavored heavily over his symptoms. It had once been the utility room. She would make sure the door was kept locked.

"In case of in no case," she would say.

I fell away from myself every now and then. I would slide right off whatever I was being held up as. I would come home and once again be the butt of my mother's love. I raised myself to a higher level of endearment to her. She decided that everybody needed an epithet, a prank appellative for the frolics ahead. Humor broke out of her in bulk. I was "lonelily unalone."

My father? His gumption went into penciled reckonings of his pension. He went otherwise unexpressed. From him I got my likeliness to tally and retire.

My bigger brother knew none of this.

Other than that, everything I say comes straight from him.

He was the one who understood the need for furniture.

"It sets you above," he said.

MEN YOUR OWN AGE

T HERE WAS SOME thrifty rigmarole I used to manage with the
ring finger of a T.A. I knew at school, when it was my sister
he claimed he was after.

This was a ring finger whose ring was tricked out with a bigger
allotment of surface novelty than you usually got with even a college ring. The thing had inlays, bossings, oversets. It was as avail-
ing an obstruction as I ever allowed that far up inside.

The college? The college was a state college with little but brick
in its nature. We came out of it in the guise of people thriveless
in pairs.

Him and my sister.

Me and a boy I later could make no lasting light of.

THAT SAID, forget them.

I was twenty-three already, in poor order among the other
clerks and mistakers in our state's junior city. We got jerked forward into the economy regardless. A man at the office had flowers
routed to my desk. In the copier room later, he joked me around
to a deplenishing kiss. But the one I moved in with breathed
more cleanly into my face. He was set on swifter sorrow, spoiling
for it. So I let myself get handed along to high-schoolers, bus-
boys with transportation, escapeways.

THEN TWENTY-FIVE, and thickened out, but you could still see a little of me around the eyes, the fitting mouth. I was off and on with an illustrator. He had the bottom half of a house and soon all the blazonry of that new disease.

He perspired and shrank.

It had to be closed-casket.

Then an immediate cleanout of his fair-haired porn before his parents and sister had their dullard turn at the shirts, the charms.

I moved into a cheesily carpentered apartment house and within days was timing my baths to the unpeaceful baths a neighbor on the other side of the wall was giving her toddler son. He would slap brattily at the water, and I would follow suit — accepting the threats, hogging scolds through the sweating tile. I otherwise kept my own counsel and did not answer the door, the intercom, the phone.

RESOLVED, THEN POOH-POOHED:

That the body is far too big a place.

Or that it's actually just the same two frivolled, sex-sickened places every time I get there.

I WAS GOING for total strangers, men methodically unfamiliar, unrememberable, in clammy concisions of limb after limb. I patrolled my body for purplements, lesions; found only the ordinaria of dim good health. And I bought a radio, one that pulled in stations from farther away. I listened to call-in programs for the gist of the distant gripe. One night it was incivility, and prices. I huddled together some examples of my own — six-fifty for five tablets that hardly smartened the bathwater; twenty-three for some jarred froth that returned little of my old gloss. I picked up the phone, dialed the long distance, was soon talking perfect, morbid sense to the screener.

"You called earlier tonight," she said.

A TRICK I LEARNED: alternate your late lunches between one restaurant and another—but just those regular two. Keep it up long enough for the counterpeople at each place to hurry to smug, merciful certitude that you're in there every single day.

You've doubled the mark you leave on the town.

You're coupled.

I WAS WHAT—thirty-one?

Let this sound better: I was cozying up to whatever was nothing to people. A loose string on the sleeve of someone's work-week sweater? I would pick it off unnoticed and give it place, keepsaken privilege, *perpetuance*, behind a window in my wallet.

That's how I hauled people off. I divided them from their lives one fiber at a time.

THEN THE MEN your own age start passing fussily into ugliness. You can point to exact places where death is already imbibing them.

Women, even the older ones, no longer seem that big a step down.

I took the ribbing and pursued myself into a few.

The first and second were swanking drunks of splendid wasted education and an abiding antagony of eye. The third did not feel up to my actual idle friction.

People are picky about any tribute they will take.

OR WAIT:

To make things easier on people, try looking at them from on high. Straight down. Then they're mainly hair and swollen waist, but mostly just the headway of their pointing shoes.

Which is to say: I married at forty-two.

The first letup in the reception and I was upstairs again, picking over the pews—programs left behind, mostly. Notes had been exchanged on a thumb-marked blank back page:

"Think he even knows who women are?"

"Low blows today at least reach a certain altitude."

Quick question: my wife?

She was slow-legged and bound to me only loosely in household hindsight already. I kept bumping into her in rooms lit only by night-lights. There was a circle of friends she said she would not give up—a thick-packed circle that went round and around in its fumings under our roof.

One day the circumference lost its give.

Thing just snapped.

Wound itself around one of the women, the least hurried to alarm.

Then my wife trying to part her from it, and the two of them fallen into each other's arms. Not "Here we finally are," but "Look, you know me better."

I learned to stir a finger in them both.

MY FINAL BEST FEATURE

I WAS GOING to lay off those years for a change, but here were
people in what might as well have been asking attitudes, and
from the whole of what I might have told them, I said only that
in me they had yet another girl who had gone as far as she could
get in life without somebody else's body to back her up, but I
for one had at least come early into the sense, thank goodness,
to keep a book open in front of me at all times, a heavyweight
paperback I was not so much reading as working a different, less
stable shape onto, putting leisurely violences into the turning of
pages so that when I was through with a book it was a lopsided
thing, something far atilt that could be pointed to, publicly, as
an example of someone's having stuck something out, and then
one morning I fed myself far enough into the population until I
came to a like-sized, schoolworn girl doing just such pointing, a
girl a little unpretty but with a heart dangerously in use behind
the buttony blouse, and the way the two of us instantly took to
each other gave us a leg up on marriage—we each set out hours
for the other to fill with just shy breathing, pinned hopes to the
ribbonry we hung wherever there were bulks of hair further discoverable upon us, feigned a unisonal swoon whenever a forearm
of either one of us was by chance drawn forward finally against

the unsleeved upper arm to produce, at the shadow-lined seam, a
mouth, surely, an unbiting mouth, which, were it to break into a
murmur, would let everything between us be a lesson to us – for
most of what any two people of that age together might do (we
were each, you see, a drowned-out, undominant twenty-three),
most of what they manage in the way of advancing the loveliness in each other, was in sorry, well-known fact addressed to,
aimed at, an unseen and unknown but counted-on third party
(it was the only progress we could see a point to), and the girl
and I were now looking to each other for a glimpse of who that
person might turn out to be; and for me, soon enough, it was
a man I was sitting only a handbreadth away from on a bus, a
thick-mouthed man in need of an underling right away, who led
me from the bus and down an off-cutting street and into a dark-
ceilinged building, where he showed me to the plasticized outer-
coat I was to wear while doing the rudimental cabinet chemistry
itself; and that should have been the extent of things, but the
man brought me home to say hello to the sister he lived with,
a woman bearing victorious versions of the man's off-sloping
chin, his wide-set nostrils, his gristly ears, and the two of them,
brother and blinking sister both, were pounding away from their
forties under one roof with only a shared kitchen between them,
the sister a little more under the weather, hoarse, watery of eye;
and in no time the sister and I were impartible, and even though
there was a voice she used solely on her brother (a sharp, finite
voice that put things straight up into the falsifying affirmative
whenever he asked whether she was all settled in for the night),
and a different voice altogether for persons who brought things
to the door (this one bracing, salutatious), she had a further
voice reserved uniquely for me, a duplexity of voice, complex
in address, which might have sounded, up top, to be saying only
"He pushes you too hard" or "I should see to supper," but which,
if you went straight to what was lowermost in it, was saying,
"Catch my cold, get yourself knocked up by the snot of it, feel
it fill you roundly out, carry it around inside of you, bring the

thing to term, blow out a mucousy umbilical string, be sure to have saved every sluttery tissue, because I am going to come to you in demand"; and it was not long afterward that she packed the brother off to a faraway bachelorship so the two of us could pass some agreeable, willinghearted months as a close-set couple, keeping each other looking looked-after, building the world up with our home truths and sore points, ready-handed, for instance, in our agreement that a man was just a frame from which a single useworthy but renounceable thing was suspended; she let out the prediction that we would be turning up eternally in each other's endearances in new, unprompted, uncurbable ways; and then one night, after some errands had removed her from the house for a run of days, she began wondering aloud whether our intimateness, agreeable as it might still seem, was in fact just a fluke accord of matching dank genitalia, whether the worst of life in fact gets its start when you are attaching feelings not to other persons but to feelings those persons have already put out of themselves, whether I had not yet come into the discovery that if one truly knew what one was doing with one's eyes, people did not actually look like what they looked like, men of course above all. The invitation to the wedding shower was forwarded to what was now my forwarding address.

THE LAST PLACE I stopped was out in the sticks, at the weld of some peewee tributary highway and another Old Airport Road. I found a couple of low buildings—a news agent's, a sistering sandwich shed. In the sandwich shed a blackboard listed drink flavors; chairs were paired badly around the few tables there were. I did not discourage a slump-breasted woman from piecing some beef together in a sandwich for me, and when she made mention of a basin of wash-water in case I wanted to rinse my hands, I wandered over to it, let my fingers while away some of the graying suds. That was when I noticed a kind of jumble shop—a few shelves and racks, really—toward the back of the place, with grab bags, lunch-sized paper bags stapled thoroughly shut at the throat and labelled, in orchid crayon, "Boy – backward," "Boy – receding," "Boy – scotched," "Girl – earliest teenhood," "Girl – done without," and so on. They were going for a dollar apiece; I bought just two: "Girl – personal life" and "Girl – beauty problems." The things within went through the fingers of one hand while the fingers of the other brought the bite-marked sandwich toward my mouth, then took it away from me again.

I went next to the news dealer's. On the floor, just inside the doorway, some tablet-paper leafletry, pamphletary curiosities, one-of-a-kind newssheets, had been weighted down with rocks. *The Stairstep Complainer* one was called, and there was *The Bedstead Unfortunate*, and *The Housetop Crier*, and *The Storm-Cellar Early Riser*; there were *The Porch-Lamp News Minder*, *The Hat-Rack Disastrist*, *The Doorstop Detractor*, *The Haulageway Daily Flare*. The window where you were supposed to pay was just a glassless rectangle cutting through the wall and into the kitchen of the sandwich shed, and when I asked how much for the papers, it was the woman from before who said, "Whatever you think is fair." I laid a five-dollar bill on her palm, then noticed a girl – I will call her a girl – standing suddenly by my side. "You bought all my papers," she said in a voice straining its way upward again from the big, killing, pubertal drop. There was just jacketing over her bare legs – it was one of those men's lightweight things (she had plunged her hips through the neck of it, worked the zipper up as far as it could be made to go, sashed the unfilled sleeves around her waist). An overlarge, gray-gone T-shirt, a man's as well, was draped stolewise over the shoulders. The line of her arm could be followed in either direction – all the way past the wrists, wreathed with shreddy, brick-colored rubber bands, to the finespun fingers, if you needed a preference, or back to the well-boned, shivery shoulder. As for the heights of her: the hair up top was short and stickied until it was barbed-looking, prickled up, and there was a skimming of fainter hair already on the upper lip, the chin. The eyes: the eyes were faithworthy eyes already getting a jump on how things would stand between us after the difficult, intermediate minutes.

And the Adam's apple—it seemed to push itself out even farther after each certain and unnervous swallow. Someone, then, who in no small part had unlikened herself blow by blow from spoilsport parents—"fuckards" was the word that would emerge for them—to become a one-girl show of hands for me alone.

For inside of a quarter-hour she had walked me to the house and up to a room whose walls were covered with crayoned skyline—big, upstricken rectangles for the buildings, little dark squares for the undisclosive windows—and over to the confining bed, where she said, "No, wait, this won't have been where it was." She escorted me past a sewing room, a utility room, a storage room, and into what I took for the parents' bedroom, onto the lofty bed of it. I must have been thinking that anything and everything fingerable on her body was keyed, pardonably, to something still unowned on mine, because before long I set my hand down on a curve of her leg, just shy of where the kneecap horizoned off. In answer, she sent an arm out flatwise onto my lap. There was a downthrow of emotion in the room, and before I even took hold of what was least obscurable on a girl of that sort, the thing had already gone withoutwards, grown away from her as far as it could go. Like most of what I had known of the world, there was a perfect, low-road way for it to take inside me. How small of me, yes, or how samely, but the way an only child becomes only an adult, the deep red I was turning became, sight unseen, my final best feature.

THE LEAST SNEAKY OF THINGS

THERE WERE STRIDES being made in human error, and it was middle-school arithmetic five columns wide he had been hired to teach with a couple of stumpy, yellow, mortal chalks, though that was not the half of it. He had been told not to fraternize with the staff, but the women among them would look him over and put a little something forward of themselves – an arm taken up with an enhancive, practiced fidgetry, perhaps – and then give him the full, accumulated thinking behind it. Only one of them will come into much value here. This was a woman with a rutted forehead, and bare forearms gone velummy from the crossings and recrossings, and glasses that did not give you her eyes at anything like their true size. She rucked her face up at him in the entranceway one morning and said, "Have a high opinion of anything?"

The day came, in short order, when he presented her with a splinty segment of a homemade ruler he had fashioned inchily from guitarwood. (He showed her a tonic discomfort to be had by slipping the thing onto the insole of her flat, murky shoe just before the foot itself returned.)

Then a cinder-gray eraser one had to operate wheelwise. (This she appointed, pendant-style, to the already intricated chains engirdling her neck, all the better to outcompass the strawberry mark hard by the collarbone.)

And one of those all-in-one drawing aids, a thing that was at bottom a protractor, which is to say only that there was a protractor set centrally into the clear plastic sheet of it, but the whole works was pranked up with off-curving flourishes and cut-out circles the diameter of practically any fattening finger. (To take hold of the thing almost anywhere, as she was quick to do, was to become a carnivaller for at least the clinched, worldly instant.)

At best, in other words, the man got himself shooed into marriage, married in fact into disease, but it wasn't disease that took her off, it was some sick-abed she fell in with, and what mattered most remainingly was a cushion she prepared for him not long before she left: it was a squarish cushion, big enough to fall asleep atop if you balled yourself up just right, and she had covered the thing anew with blithely striped fabric of a coarse, heavyweight, farewell sort. For weeks afterward, this cushion was the man's lone seat. Then one night a seam came open. A tiny unparting of the threads at first, and then a liplike tear that took on howling length and width as weeks went loudly out. What showed through wasn't the siftings, the stuffings, he would have expected, but an earlier coverature, a dated floral patterning – plushier, staled – that was trouble to touch because of how thoroughly it mongered up the previous, unhelpful life of hers: the off years, the fair shares of misdevotion, the hard water and dirtier looks, the last straws and accelerating changes of heart. It was all there, confidential and contagioned in what he took for rotting cotton.

Only two further things need saying to clamp down even worse.

The first is simply that there was a pencil he set out, in secret, early-bird provocation, for the other teachers to reach for, then put down again, unstolen, on the deep-pocked countertop of the full-house faculty lounge. It was a worktable pencil he had sharpened to a fetching, irresistible half of its original span, and he had gone and scribblingly reduced the point of it to a long-suffering, well-rounded bluntness, and he had then left it to catch and collect as much as it could of his fellows, because in no time even the least sneaky of things will have already been handled awfully, will have drawn onto themselves a commonwealth of squandered touch: anything eventually sports the lonelihood of people who could no longer keep their hands to themselves. Why then own up to having any further unsanitary use for the people themselves when you already owned so much of what had gone ruiningly through their hands?

The other, final matter is that in the classroom thereafter he no longer had the heart to insist that his pupils "carry" any leftover digits from the rightmost column of workbook numerals to the summit of the previous one. He instead had the pupils laying the surplus numbers aside ("These loose, glutting, ridiculable tidbits of ongoing arithmeticizing" they were now to be called): the pupils were to set them out on the bed of a separate piece of paper, the backmost sheet of the dwindling, unlined tablet, and then he would lead the pupils in tearing the sheets cleanly free, would recite the grave, tribulationary instructions on just how every numberful sheet was to be folded into a weak-bodied box, and then each was to be walked single-file up to the desk so that the teacher might give it the completive tuck and fold. His touch was the touch of a precisioner—and the boxes were stacked flimsily tall on his desk as a wall against parents who were overlappingly dissatisfied, who showed up in jolty patrols of two or three to pull their sons, their troublable daughters, from his classes. But looks alone would have told you that the children had been put, at most, only a little further forward on the vanguard of everything going by the board.

MELTWATER

HERE WAS A MAN, he claimed, who had caught his life early and already was bottoming on the parts of the world available to him, and I remember saying, "It won't happen again," and then the two of us broke away from the line of urinals in careful, patient union. I followed him to the building where he lived – a free-standing single room, a garage-sized office, as things would have it. He explained that the most to be expected of anyone in his circumstance (the world was hard put to keep itself looking full) was to have both a girlfriend and a boyfriend, in hopes that the two would cancel each other out and leave him at the center of an enlarged, more compassing loneliness. I had nothing further to do with him other than getting the people's names and looking them up.

Of the boyfriend I have little to pass along, except that he turned out to be my equal in the overintelligibility of his face – teeth the color of margarine, I'm afraid; eyes that rivalled the lights; a rampant, unlimited nose. There was a garland of dark hair growing around his neck and shoulders (he was shirtless the little while I knew him), and there was much talk – rumorous murmur, really – all that week in the apartment below his: a pair of voices, male and discussive, that got pitched even lower as they

were channeled up through the floorboards and the deep carpet-
ing on which the man and I lay after all our trouble. Sometimes
I could make out a third voice downstairs, that of a contestant
female, just a visitor, no doubt, and a laugher. I never got to meet
her and to this day still suspect that she had a smoky hood of
unshampooed hair and the sleep-buckled arms of a quitter. But
this boyfriend: had I sought merely another reminder that everything always gets stuck being slightly more than just itself, that
objects flourish in the thick of their own innuendoes, and that
the trick, therefore, is not to look directly at any one thing but
instead to concentrate hard on the haze environing it, until whatever it is, the form emerging thereunder, wobbles a little further
within its outline and becomes separable, easily chased out? For
I came away with nothing more than one of his combs, a largely
ornamental one, the crown of his toilet, and another new reason
to keep from touching all the old things.

The girlfriend, on the other hand, was in some sort of accel-
erated rehab. I slipped in on family day and sat by her side on a
lawn that sloped toward the expressway. She was undodging and
level-chested in her baggy sundress, and she necklaced her arms
around my shoulders to confide that she had a private room and
that these were merely the sick days and personal days she had
long had coming to her, taken now in one salutary lump. Afterward, assisted out of each other's clothes, we displayed ourselves
at full length in the coarsening fluorescence of her room (I remember a port-wine stain enriching the goosefleshy preserve
beneath her left breast). By day's end, she had already bargained
for an early release (she had some vague, undefiable kind of pull),
and I came to stay at her house. The next morning, she was back
at her office, and I began humbling each day down into heart-
drowning dozes of roughly equal length. After every one of them,
I would turn myself around, unespoused, on the uppermost
bedclothes (alone, I drew back none of the covers, seldom resorted to a pillow) and throw in my lot with what I was already
in the middle of.

For the woman had a son, a collegian in his late teens, who was mostly at work or in class, and who went around the house in exactingly parted hair: the parting was a coercionary line, an unfailing divider, that I came to reverence as a segment of a much longer line that I formed a niggly segment of myself: a line that travelled by inchmeal through unpined-for bodies and spreadless, low-pitched towns and now and again hit an improving stride and was manifestable, broken up anew, in the vivid transection of a boy's head of hair or in the outgoing, eminent prolongation making a fresh, last-minute mess of my crotch. The line, as I thus set about reconstituting it, directed me, soon enough, to the boy's room; and it was in the course of making a first search of that room (prospecting in the high-posted dresser, the desk with its deep drawers, the heavy-lidded hamper, as soon as the boy and his mother were both at last out of the house) that I turned up his pornography, the little there was of it, in a night table that opened, cupboardlike, from the front. It was a slender magazine, a one-shot, a "special" dedicated to I forget precisely which partialism, and I dallied in the drab thing until I reached the page most singularized by the boy's touch—a recto, ten pages or so from the rear, marked off with a batch of proprietary thumbprints and depicting an ignorable girl, foul-eyed and recumbent in pajamal diaphaneities, one hand raised unshieldingly above the triangular murk showing through at her center.

It was the backdrop of the photograph, though, that brought me up short: a remote, all but vanishing blue—one of those decrescent, lesser blues, with nothing the least spirituous or skyey in the cast of it, yet crisal, crisic, just the same: a blue that did not so much give out on the world as give up on it (but without tossings, without vehemences!) and that sent me, almost at once, and without a sweater or a shave, to the paint store closest by. The salesman spread out a fan of color charts, then fed them one by one into my hands. I charged through the charts with disappointment until, on a thick, palette-shaped card of enamels

("finishers," the salesman called them), I came up against something close to a match: meltwater it was called, and it had to be
whipped up specially in a countertop mixer that gave off a tem-
perate, alto hum. I came away with a sploshing gallon can aswing
from each hand, and a stirring paddle and a paintbrush in my
back pocket; but that first night (an early-autumn night sloppy
with rain and coiling traffic), I merely committed a dauby speci-
men of the paint to my fingernails and arrived, unventilated and
ready to catch him out, this "commuter," at the dinner table. The
boy, however, was unfazed and unrecognizing as I sent before him
with my upcast fingertips the bowls of stew, the gleaming salads.
I remember a notable excurvature of muscle, not unbecoming,
beneath the snug drapery of the boy's short sleeve each time he
accepted a dish.

The next morning, with the run of the house once more, I re-
gained the boy's room and, this time, with my paint at the ready,
let myself into one of his spiraled notebooks ("SOC SCI," he had
written in prissed, lessonly caps on the cover) and at deserving
length skimmed my laden brush down the margin of the page
where he had left off. (The notes had been recorded in soft-pen-
ciled, back-slanting abbreviations that seemed on the brink of
retreating from the page.) The boy came home from work, vanished into his room, and, I gathered sorrily, went untormented
about his assignments.

A couple of mornings later, with all the windows in the boy's
room thrown open to a low-going, unmetropolitan sky, I gave
a slapping introductory coat to the baseboards. That evening, I
arranged a quick dinner for all three of us (the boy unperplex-
ing the salad I had stocked with bouillon cubes, tindersticks of
pasta, enfoiled chocolate exotica; the woman recompressing her
slipshod sandwich), and afterward parked myself in the living
room, nose lowered alertly into a thickset volume of the scarlet
household encyclopedia. But, once more, whether through simple imperception or the killjoy composure of a born flirt, the boy
gave no sign—merely kept up the tit-tat of his lap typewriter as

he harbored words for his "comp." The woman was at her phone for the night, and as on all such occasions, I took up the incontinent crusade against my body, trying to clear my face by going after the late-day hair appreciating on the chin, the cheeks, abstracting the hairs one by one with a slant-tipped tweezer, enough of them to cumulate into broken lines down my shirtfront and onto a double page of the encyclopedia spread now across my thighs. There was a bulblet at the root-end of every hair; and certain of these, when subjected to an experimental pressure of the thumb, could be made to excrete a dark, private ink that left a tiny smouch on the page. (I had so little else to show.)

The next afternoon (I had slept well into its steep-rising shadows, because, come night, almost everything was costing me my sleep: the almost coppery taste of the dry heat as it reached my open mouth, the woman's least turnings on her span of the bed as my life kept pivoting filthily off her own: I was always on pain of waking to the snottery monotone of her snores or other earthly maneuvers of hers – and yet with what whispery concern I would test the nip-and-tuck vowels of her name: Sael!) – the next afternoon, I applied harrying fluences of blue paint to a zone of stucco above the boy's bed until I was satisfied that my jittering brushwork had yielded a sightworthy, window-sized rectangle.

This, apparently, was as much as it was going to take, for after dinner the boy interrupted my reading, escorted me to his room, assumed a vibrant position on the brim of his bed, and conducted me by suggestive, irregular swallows into his hardship. It started with the car that gave him no peace (it was slow to get going, he said, then squirted of its own accord into traffic that always took its time to part), and the shortcomings of commuter life (the "dormitorium," to hear him describe it, was not the bricky, box-shaped residence hall of the sort I could still call up from remembered youth but, instead, a far-reaching yet indefinite complicacy of stone and shaded glass whose central escalators, I gathered, would afford the "nonresident" an aggrieving

vista of students dead to the world in humid pairs and three-
somes on the marbled slabs of groined galleries that were ranged
about the base of a foggy rotunda), and his boss (a franchiser
given to intimate insanitations, scratch-paper threats), and, finally, "girlettes," "feminatrices," as the boy termed them, and
their inconvenient, pinksome anatomies. I explained to the boy
that in my day we had counted ourselves lucky if, once a month,
rummaging through the family ragbag, we turned up one of
our fathers' forsworn T-shirts and hacked off the sleeves and the
neckhole and then pulled the remains down, sacklike, over our
hips until the hem got as far as our knees—and that, in sum, midway down a body, man's or woman's alike, the trouble is always
original and always suits. Here I fixed a hand on the boy's upper
leg and spoke, at last, of bachelorisms, slipslops of the heart,
and, most of all, how to hold it, the troubler, aloof from yourself,
how to regard it at most as a guest of the body and not a per-
manence on it, because the truth is that the thing did not origi-
nate from within you but in fact grew onto you from afar—you
merely hosted it. I thus came into a rash knowledge of the boy's
differentiae—distant, backside moles he could have only guessed
at, the tensed setting of every rung of his ribs.

On the floor, a skyline of furniture curving above us, I set him
forward in his larger life just a little.

(Days thus passed under the woman's nose.)

An hour or so before the woman returned from work late each
afternoon, the boy and I would now share a confidential fore-
meal of chocolate bric-a-brac and a thinning, sepia-toned liquid
that trafficked from a high bottle to a tumbler I had taught the
boy to keep upright in the blowsy yarn of the carpet. His hands
were newly productive, formatting dinner napkins into bon-
nets, depressing cookie batter into shatterable hearts. There were
other gustoes of mine the boy would not soon escape. And I told
him to forget words from here on in—that once you got even
one of them out, a whole cortege of others would be bringing
up its stinking rear.

Early one night, the woman came suddenly from behind my chair and said, "You better would've not've." I craned my neck to meet her halfway. There was an alien, liquorous tilt to her features.

You only get way too many chances, I must have put in, because I remain of the enormous opinion.

But I "walked."

I came, in due course, to the food court of a mall (for the world was yet to be taken by mouth) and worked myself toward the Chinese bay: behind the counter was an overblooming, low-hatted girl, a blonde (youth is vast!). I ordered by number and presently accepted a routine, rimmed density of chicken and vegetables. At my table afterward, devoting myself to the meal, narrowing my gaze to the limits of my plate, I discovered amid stray splinters of fried rice a rich, characterical hair: it was more than an inch and a half in uncurled longitude and of darksome human gloss. I had not had a look at the food-prep station or the cook (they had scrims nowadays, dividers), but I pictured somebody down on everyone else's luck.

For this hair—there was a body surely recoverable from it: putty in my hands and no great shakes.

HEIGHTS

SHE HAD always kept up an interest in the avocations of the familiar. One could return to a room, after all, and find that paper, ordinary paper, had since been folded until it was bladed and held danger. Or one could pass into a kitchen (for one had been away, sullyingly, again) and descry, on the stove, mere finger-breadths from the oniony ebullition in a saucepan, a tablespoon already beginning a career as food itself. If she fitted the bowl of the spoon into her mouth, there would be the discovery that the stainless steel had a filling and satisfying taste all its own.

She married, in other words, a fellow who had decided that women alone could ever be man enough for him now. He would entertain the pressure of her hand on his cheek and have his blood tapped and inspected once a month. One night, the man wanted to have people over, people more like himself. She sat in the bedroom and listened to the men's voices, thick and inept, playing with what had already been said, making good on her misgivings.

Or so I gathered as much from the deteriorating alphabets of her doodles, and from the faces with which she kept resoiling paper for me to have to regard—shapes of accumulating unease one minute and slaphappiness the next, each finally evicted from the page with jerked expunctions of her eraser. For this woman was no gabber like the ones they usually put next to me now that they had us working two to a table. The regular pencil looked heavyset, out of scale, between her hurrying fingers.

She was a worthy opponent of herself. Gray fillings discriminable in the thin teeth during a rare, airy yawn. A depleted comeliness to her face. Not one word out of her, ever. But one day a switch of her hair fell finally across my sleeve. I forget who followed whom out onto the landing.

We sat in her car because the passenger seat of mine had been stuffing itself all along with steadfast pilings, elevations, of newspapers, circulars, discarded cardboard. Her voice was melodial but economic. She explained that her mother had always claimed that hours weren't bait, something laid out to trap with, but to her mind, time was still waiting to get itself told. Thus her hand came to rest so livingly on my own.

We became another arm-swinging pair waging walks on the town, fooling with heights.

I CRAWL BACK TO PEOPLE

LEATRICE

THERE WAS a kind of woman you could spend weeks with, months even, and never get it settled to your satisfaction whether she was on the mend or not yet finished being destroyed. This one was no different, only younger than I by a couple or so years, though on a second or third life already. We were together one spring, briefly, tickledly, and then it came to her – in a dream, in a diary entry; I forget – that I would not be having her very much longer. Then I lost her altogether. I remember the tears she provided in a waiting area at the airport before she left, and how she insisted on being the one to make the trip to a snack bar for some napkins to blot the tears, and how it looked like little more than perspiration she was wiping away when she got back. Then she fell in line to board, and I went out to seek my car. I lay across the seat until I heard a plane take off and could satisfy myself that it might have been hers. I drove back to the city. In a couple of days I was already picking her out by the piece here and there on other people, because people came to hand on other people or drifted up out of one another availably. There was always some scrap of her arising usefully in passing on somebody or other.

What I mean is that people shaded into each other pretty easily, and all I had to do was find her somewhere there in the gradients.

I found tender burlesques of her hair on one girl, and exactly the scoop of her underarms on another, and approximations of her forearms on an uncavorting kid of seventeen. I could get him to feed me the seizing feel of her sometimes.

In fact, it was this kid, a high-schooler, that I mostly got her dwindled down to by the end of that first summer.

The attic he lived in was underbeloved by the rest of his family, so we could generally count on privacy. If a parent stuck a head in the room, I fell back on instant dramatics of mid-level math, pad-and-pencil finesse left over from taunted years at the commonwealth college.

The kid showed me his middle-school yearbook, his tapes, some bitter, unvisionary pornography.

He had a big dictionary that contained mostly disappointments—"bottle tit," for one. It was just some dim, skinny bird nesting in the holes of trees overseas.

"Are troops the individual guys or bunches of guys all huddled together?" he seemed to wonder. He had balmed lips and novel, weary whiskerage that looked crafted on.

So I took to frocking this and that onto the kid—got him gowned in a bedsheet, skirted with a bath towel. Brought him a sleeveless thing for him to slink deep within. Got his starter razor buzzing above the ankles, taking out the blond dither along each shin.

I milked his arms for further thrill of her farewell.

CAULEN

HE ALREADY had a way, when passing alone through an entrance, of keeping the door held open a little behind him, in event of a follower.

He was the type not ruinable ordinarily.

But I knew what to buy him—blood-colored underwear, man-tailored shirts from women's stores.

Knew how he could be stood to outpourings of infallible citric alcohols.

Knew I could get him to where I guess he expected only better things to push up through what he already thought of me.

So at last he was professing it—an excruciated fellowship I would have some share of.

TOGETHER, HOUSED, we banged each other up with contestable affections.

He had grated good looks.

He cooked savvily on a berserk four-burner.

A few hairs of his came loose during the bustling solitude of a shower. They stuck to a block of soap already claiming several of mine.

We were that much together even in toiletry.

THERE WERE EXACTLY two bars in our catchwater town upstate. I forget why I started sending him off alone.

One was a warehouse revived for dancing. The other bar had only stools, in my clumsy opinion.

He came home with something against wallets—something about how the way to get one thing to belong to another should not have to require putting them side by side in a leather packet and then sitting on them until, if you wanted just one, you had to practically peel it apart from the other. It bothered him that it took a rear end at rest to make sure that things would stick together.

THINGS CAME and went on his face, his back, in pustular debuts, crusting retreats.

Some days his hair stole over him differently.

It riffed out more racily under his arms.

IN HIS DEFENSE? You could work only so long at a furniture outlet before minding it that every sofa and chair was plushly, or hard-armedly, dramatizing its lack of a suitable sitter.

Every stick of furniture was a history of spurning asses.

You get better and better at dialing down the light to the point where passersby decide the place is probably closed.

He later sold phones and had glum dominion over a teenager with repatterned teeth and a rubber band bangled swankly over his wrist.

For a couple of weeks, I commanded repeat condolences from our pallid little crowd.

KELL

THE IDEA WAS to marry lightly, not go overboard or be private about things, just let affections string out as they might. I expected to see streamers of feeling coloring up the air between us.

Each of us said: "I'm not going anywhere."

She was none too grubby for having dug herself out from other people. I could smell the same dud soap on her always.

I was sometimes by her side while she shopped. Her "Thank you very much" to the change-tendering cash-wrap girls always had in it an acknowledgment of applause.

We lived without onslaught. The days did not clobber us or break new ground. She did some kind of surefire statisticizing during the day. Collected informations, forced them through a formula until they came out pestled, floury.

She would sweat off her makeup over dinner.

Ruffled nostrils, wear and tear in the eyes, pressuring escalations of a competitive pink in the complexion—her body wasn't pioneering anything, it wasn't hectic in its decrepitude: she wasn't shading off ahead of schedule. Her vaginal efficiency was unchanged.

But more and more ornaments got hung from her. There was fierce hoopla in all those boostering units of chainwork and chatelaine.

She began vanishing into jumpsuits, quilted coveralls.

I would say something, and she would chop or wrinkle it into something else, but she was never far from wrong—neither of us could have ever been saying much more than "I won't keep you."

I understood, but then there was a shimmy to my understanding, and I no longer exactly could follow.

FAISAL

THERE WERE HOLES in what I felt for people, and it was through these holes that I slid finally toward this fourth.

I bummed a touch from her in the subway. I let the touch aggrandize itself unquietly.

I moved to her steep-streeted city downstate.

She decided I was a deserver.

She was a woman of punctual life-tides, ate right, had suffered at all the right hands. She had a drafty manner and jewelry that tailed off asymmetrically from her ears in a show of what looked like sugar. She had been grossing all of this great, capering beauty for something like twenty-six years. We did the giveaway pharmaceuticals of the season. We went out with her friends, busy-headed kids her own age, to crack up over menu English. I loved her sundrily and all at once.

There was, to start, the givenness of her bare arms, and legs you could pick out of a dress and follow all the way down to the pewtery hue of the toenails.

Childhood, teenhood, were still refrigerating inside her. I could make out the timid din of who she had already been, a hum of harms hardly done.

The question put to me by skeptics was: "What is she doing with you?" I was swift to answer: stapling personal papers together, breathing providently in her broad-hearted sleep, bearing junk mail straight from the mailbox to the trash cans in front of her building.

"No," they would say. "What does she see in you?"

I told them I was doubling for somebody. It's hard not to be standing in for people jokingly slow to show. Go-betweens impart important impromptu breadth to any population, keep cities backed up and abrim.

They would say: "How can this be good?"

I said it's called middle age because everything is just circling around you now. You're at the discouraged center. Why should it all of a sudden be any ruder to reach?

She had never been to a drive-in movie, so I withdrew an address from the phone book, drove us to some gravelly outer county. There was one shack where you bought the tickets, another where you bought unsatisfactory snacks. The screen was a folly of peeling panels. "I'm not your pillow," she taught me early in the first picture. During intermission, I directed my twinkling, postponed piss into a metal trough. Through the wall I listened to her relaxed, sassing abundance in the bowl. No flush, no siss of faucets afterward. In stinting rain on the way back to town, she complained that my windshield wipers were too loud.

The doubters said, "It's over, isn't it?," or gave us maybe another week.

The way she left things when she was done with them – narrow ranks of cutlery, a high-raised figurinal telephone, dish after dish of jotted chocolates – the weight seemed thrown around in them differently, they looked plummety or fickle in their molecularity, they harbored her touch with too much rumpus.

It got harder to get her arm through mine.

One afternoon she mentioned a brother somewhere else who lived on one floor and was host to a lonesome federation of straight-backed chairs, pull-up chairs, TV chairs. It was time for her to see him again and be ready for what he was facing. I gave her a lift to the airport. In the car, she lowered a balled fist onto my lap and explained that we were set up much too differently in our bodies; that there were no lasting or reliable handholds on each other; that I would turn up something nicely remindful of her dry-boned elbows or collisive knees on somebody nearer my own age; that the xoxoxoxoxoxoxoxos given as sign-offs in the few, close-written letters she had sent me were actually tallies, each X standing of course for a mistake I had made, every O just my final score.

I have probably got her features collated all wrong in memory anyway.

I have no doubt given freehand failings to the line of the mouth, leaving the lips figgled, defaulting.

Jollied a lone, focal mole along to the slope of the nose.
Undarkened the down at the bounds of the cheek.
Brought the eyes to unfinal idle crisis.
The world has since figured her into its fixed emotional fare.
I count on others to cough valiantly, or turn on aquarium
pumps, run fans, when I think to bring her up.

DAUGHT

No SOONER had my husband and I fixed up a place of our own than a book arrived on the well-meaning subject of landlordry. I was in no mind to read it, but I interested myself in the graces and attractions of its manufacture: it was a loose-jointed but otherwise well-kept old thing, and if I thumbed ahead to the midmost pages, a little nether passageway opened welcomingly between the arched edges of the signatures and the inner strip of the spine, and I could either admit a finger into this hollow and then shut the book to feel some barely favorable pressure, or I could bring it up to my eye scopewise and enjoy a narrowing, exclusive view of the ashtray serving as a caddy for my thermometer, perhaps, or of the chromatic strata of pills in a see-through canisterette—I was not much troubled that things could now and then look so suddenly, relievedly, independent. Still, the stacked pages, however stale, must have exhaled at least enough of their purpose to influence my choice of what next to allow into my hand, because it was a plump marker and not the thermometer just this once, and it must have been big and wishful of me to think that by printing "ROOMS" (largely, coarsely) on the back of the envelope the book had turned up in, and then by tilting my little sign against the bow window, I was putting out only some benevolent, overdue description – an explanation, I mean, and not an ill-vowelled cry of availability.

As for the passing woman first to knock: if her cheeks were pock-pitten and mealy, there was a complexional rosiness in the upper reaches of her arms, which were wisely left unsleeved; and if her breasts fell inobligingly short, there was a way I could get her to sit with her knees just wide enough apart for them to see duty as a second, hardier bosom when my head needed its place for rest; and if her mouth struggled to hold in the dim, shifting masonry of the teeth when she kept letting out that she lacked "destiny, remedy, delight," there was a more opportune mouth forming at the jointure of the thigh and the calf when the leg was at last drawn in, and this one could be kissed without risk or return; and if there was anything else that did not instantly suit, there was sure to be something cater-cornered to it or not too distant that would do in a pinch and no doubt prove even warmer and more aromal in the end.

Then I must have remembered that all along I had probably just needed someone to walk in with me when I finally went around to see the teacher. Classes had let out by the time the two of us, the roomer and I, reached the high-vaulted desk up front. There was a line of transparent party tumblers near the edge of it, in one of them a razor downside up in scummage, in another a toothbrush abob in a streaky solution I trusted was recycled mouth-rinse – by then her fingers and mine had to have been braided together even tighter, I can at least now hope.

A towel was draped around his neck, and he was guiding a cake of soap dryly across his forehead. He took us in with his full nostrility. His shirt was off, so it was all to the good that he was heavy enough for the vaccination mark on his arm to have swollen out to practically a sunburst, glazy-looking and something to keep my eyes away from his. He did not think to ask about my lady friend, but he wanted me to know that although the boy had nothing against the "material" *per se*, he would lay aside the lessons and pass most of his days in the lavatory; that on the

walls and door of the stall he favored, the boy had rendered cred-
itable side views of bunk beds, four-posters, foldaways, cots; that
the custodian, who was getting ready for a move and needed to
dispose of things anyway, had donated to the stall a plant stand
and a floor lamp and a parcel of foam-white carpet, which in its
day must have surely kept guests on tiptoe in even their most al-
legiantly cleansed stocking feet; that visitors were admitted only
one by one, and after they emerged (this one's pullover now
inside out or smelling of smoke, that one's arm sinking beneath
its new load of roped jewelry), they pleaded for time—

But I cut him off, either on the principle that they're no good
until you've got them to where they rule the roost, and then
they're worse, or else on its opposite, which could still keep me
bullied into believing that somebody should always at the least
be the one being wooed.

"For your information," I said, "it's my daughter, anyway, that
I'm gunning for."

He had started poking his sunny arm into a sleeve.

"I would ask, then, whether you even have any idea of what a
daughter is," he said.

It was of course only one thing for her to chime in with "A
person, pushedly female, who daughts," and altogether another
to be first to define "daught" the way I should minutely let it stand.

IN KIND

TO HEAR ME TALK, I had been a browless child in shoes with
an expressive swoop to the lacing, and I came out of college
about the time the profs were just starting to get eerie about
grades, and after graduation, I walked out warringly into society
for a while.

This was in a town without much in the way of vicinity–just
groupings of confusable buildings and fields we were expected
to treat as parks.

I had no friends, just timid emergency contacts.

I married the second woman to come along.

The first had been clear-hearted, and hair-colored, and the few
times she spoke, it sounded as if water were running over her
words. Something was coursing through her speech that was
other than what she was saying, even when all she was saying
was: Tell me your news.

MY WIFE – in third grade, she had called her teacher at home
one night to ask what he was up to. (He said he was right that
very moment being dragged toward the door.) She was a hard-
boned girl afraid her heart would halt between beats. She went
around with her hand covering it, until somebody finally said,
"Must you always be pledging allegiance?"

Anything she related came only from this same short strip of girlhood. So one assumes, naturally, that there were years long ago set fire to, or put unsafely away into other, worldlier people. More likely, though, it was only that life had covered up her life.

BUT WHEN had either of us ever been one for bastions, strongholds?

We lived, my wife and I, in a morbid swither, and were inaccurate in our passions, and now and again frightened ourselves into feeling on the verge of something that could lead to change or at least a better examining of who we already were.

I was endlong in my enclosing forties, chumpy, rump-faced.

My tendencies boiled down to the tendency to have trouble seeing what was right in front of me, then to follow anyone else's eyes to maybe just a larger situation of noodles stymied in a dish.

I had a heart cleaned out and in need of new keep.

I LIKED TELLING people that their secrets were safe with me, but I was in fact a deadliness to them, each and severally.

I wrote stapled manuals of policy and dampened encouragement for outfits that sold "financial products." I mostly just copied, substituting "should" for "shall," then substituting "might have at some point in the past" for "definitely should have." I insisted on "she or he," then cut out the "he" altogether. All the bosses, managers, executives, decision-makers, vessels of discretion in my clamping paragraphs were female in body, female in parts.

AS FOR MY PARENTS?

They had let life drop away from them.

And I had a brother, younger. We were not close, but something must have been jumping around in his feelings for me and sometimes hit against his heart in a scrubbing way.

RATHER, THERE WAS the city you called home, and there was a companion city, a comparison town, some miles downlake, and you went back and forth between the two, working in one and living in glaring well-being in the other, or elating your family by marrying in one and buying rousing flowers for some other in the second, until a third place went up in the neutral form of tents and tarps, thank goodness. This was where I came to associate my life with my body in ways that there was definite bloodied overlap.

OR THEY JUDGE you by what you make a run for, and I made a run for a kid not even out of the district. He had thorough hair, with a blonded backstream to it, and earaches, nose aches, and no sensation at all on one side of his tongue, and his family spoke to him only through block parents or glory holes.

So which was the bad sign—that I had no influence over him, or that I came to him so often with militant doses of alleviatives I crushed with tablespoons myself?

WOMEN WERE ring fingers, toenails a pickled purple, powdered belittled features, panics laid bare on stationery, then sharpened in forthtelling agony over the phone.

My wife taught eleventh-hour math to twelfth-graders. It was just glorified arithmetic—the friction of recipe fractions, check-cashing-service subtraction. The students were imaginative nincompoops quick to petition.

I would awaken unquietly upcity, shower with some figure of fun, whoever it was. Often a colleague's son, a kid unbeaten at the comedy of his lengthening life and possessed of jabbing stops in his voice. It was a voice that dumped glassy vocabulary over the world immediate to him and his paining good nature.

The muck wouldn't get into my days until later.

I WAS OTHERWISE talked about in an interested and summarizing way.

There were uncles I saw mostly as pallbearers and peacemakers, and there were aunts who had been reared to throw themselves loftily at waning neighboring bodies in days stout with time. The grandmother on my father's side was eye-sick, dry-throated; an upheavalist in the mornings, a regretter come night. Afternoons, she took her tragedies with tweezers and reasoning.

It was my grandfather on the other side who brought the caustics to the bloodline.

MY OFFICE HAD a window, but it gave out on the corridor, not on the renewable contrarieties of the world outside, and I covered the glass with bare cardboard, though not quite completely: there was a narrow strip at the bottom through which anyone up for the bother could see clear through to where I was, often as not, leading a throwaway razor, without balm of water or foam, across a freshly despised portion of forearm, or simplifying an underarm snarl with pinking shears.

These were things I did on the job, yes, as if the job were a base, a foundation, on which I threw myself around inside myself.

Home, I was budged but unadvancing. For whole weeks what came to me in dreams went right back again into the stream of sleep, unminded.

SHE TALKED ALOUD in her dozes, this wife, though much of what got said sounded only like toasts or alerts.

The parts she had come from were mostly farms, with here and there the hardened variety of a village.

AND THAT NEIGHBOR I drank with during the stinks of summer: he was barely half my age, but his life was levelled against him in ways that made his past look ledged with trick precipices.

I could never get the chronology right—construction first, or carpentry, then the pinching year or two as a package handler, the engagement (torched) to somebody unfavorable in baby fat, then the mono, the money damages, the meatlessness and drinking, the death of a friend with whom the friendship had been veiled and failing?

I would have him over when my wife was out for sitdowns with sisters or another ireful, untiring walk before bed.

I liked the differing trueness of him when he made his mouth unwelcome to mine, and the resting eyes he had, and always that raincoat, always those annulling motions he made with the hands.

I HAD TO GET ALONG with what I could gather of myself, and what I could gather was mostly this—that I had to answer every question with a question, and it had to be: What else might you miss?

TWO CHILDREN, YES. There must have been nights when there was patience on offer in my heart, nights I sat beside them when they were still in school and could be ruled or at least feared without too much fright.

These were a sturdying girl of vague obediences, a boy hidden in his hardihood.

Their names, their first names, formed a blatty, honorary off-rhyme, I want to say.

But they must have felt buttoned into each other, those two of ours.

The excusatory note the girl had forged to her teacher: in forky penmanship, it said she had been "homesick," not "home sick."

And the boy: the climbings and depressions in his backhand posterboard alphabet were, the teacher wanted to warn, without apparent parallel.

He later shirked his gender or got himself ousted from it, and had a curt, spiking life, little of it limpid.

The girl grew up to browse herself hourly for allurements. I am getting ahead of myself if I say that a ruin shouldn't usually start out as one.

THE OUTGOING manager was having me throw together a memoir for her, a dignification, really, of any dent she might have made in things behind the partitions upstairs. She was a woman of unhurrying readiness, and anecdotes already deserting her, and scarcely enough names to go with faces, faces I let putresce and appall in pagelong sketches in the chapter on hirelings, associates, lunchmates easily fathomed. There was, for each, a paragraph of fallacious acclaim, a word on domestic conditions, and a single, fair criticism.

Myself I wrote off as a town wonder now toned down – low-spoken, overmuch of body, slow to show his undersides.

PEOPLE DID not expect to stay on in my affections, but I never really finished with anyone, never really saw them off from places they had filled.

I brought my work home, meaning I was still on the job, meaning I was athwart some notion of it.

An afternoon might feel original and culminating, or else the hours had hardly a touch of time in them.

My neighbor needed someone in front of him to express his difference from, and I was content to face his features whenever they afforded me the wide weekday arrays of his woe.

THERE WERE the beginnings of a rip in her visage, and cakier gloomings of makeup on her eyelids, but still an ingredience of sympathy in our evenings overall.

A lot of well-wishing went on just before we went to sleep, plenty of warmest regards and the like, though in remembered and confided dreams we were hurtful, encumbering, believable.

I CAN'T take it upon myself to say there weren't others, familiars for a day or two, thankless in kind. And a girl once, too, though she had seen herself formed into a woman who absorbed men only by accident, and with women was even less guiding.

AND A WORD about the house where I lived liably with this wife and these flimsily boned loved ones and whatever was kept drumming around inside them: it had several and a half baths, and was sectored into vestibules, entryways, and other prefatory thresholds. You had to take a breather from this person before reaching that one. In like manner, the big, fat lies added up.

MONTHS, AND WHATEVER else there might have been to catch or cadge; jury duty and cautions in the mail; a few more neighbors, every one of them a presentable disgrace with a body barely squarable with mine; an undegenerate but consequential blotch on the upper leg; niceties it was in my nature to deny; replies that more and more often had to begin, "If what you say is true..."

It is true that I had bought, some years back, at the one thrift store in town where men's and women's T-shirts were racked emboldeningly together, an armful of the women's things, the plainest ones, varying from the men's only in the girth and in the length of the sleeves, and under my dress shirts and sports jackets these held me closely for a decent while. I held up dearly in them, yes. I wore them to pieces.

AND THEN one whose bearings I shortly preferred to mine: he had done cruelly in school (maps were rolled down like window shades over anything he had sneaked up onto the chalkboard, the mystifying anatomies and such), and in college he had to raise just the right facts out of the chapters because the quizzes were quick and graded on machines that had to be wheeled in. He wanted me to declare him looted of youth.

It was the truth, or there at least was truth arranged around in it somewhere, or it had been true enough of somebody else, anyone approximate who had wanted to be a girl and grew up to content himself with the offsloughs of a wife ruddily losing her looks.

CASE IN POINT: whenever a large dog died, a cage even larger was left behind to fill. My friend—for I had a friend at the time I am considering, someone lonesome even in his chosen loneliness—knew somebody in just that sort of bind. The dog had been a huffy lug named after a seasoning or garnish. It had died of bloat and a heart hard to make out. My friend had the cage brought over, and we looked at the thing for a while until he thought to say, "You'll fit."

This friend locked me in certainly. There were a couple of stainless-steel bowls to be hung—one for food, the other for water—and he promised to keep both of them topped off. There was a long, shallow pan for him to slide underneath, too.

I must have let out a whimper, because he said, "You're not a dog. You're in a dog's cage."

So for a few days I felt cramped, no argument there, and my skin was waffled from the wired sides and floor, but I have only one remaining complaint. My friend one morning brought me a magazine, a jubilating weekly, and I opened it and laid it on my floor, but there was no way to read the thing. My eyes were too close to the pages. So I spread the magazine up against the side of the cage. That way, though, I was just blocking the light. I told myself to remember to tell my friend to leave the lamp on the next time he came to refresh the bowls. But I never did. The magazine was eventually in the way, and I accidentally dirtied it, and my friend brought around someone who brought in bedding from his car—oversheets and undersheets, foam-rubber stuffings, an unfrilled duvet. The two of them went to waste on each other in stages upstairs.

INSIDE OF A MONTH, I had already been living alone in a new apartment, adjusting to the parquetry and pilot lights, waiting for this to be the one time I thought better of myself and my marriage, when I began to hear, at unpredictable hours (once as late as weekday midnight), a couple of men on good terms of some stubborn sort in the apartment under mine. But whether what I was divining in these voices was the residential ease and ridicule of companions or the trucelike give-and-take of repairmen on call, I could not finally get it settled.

In sum: whether the night befell the day or vice versa, the hours of either were soon bleedable for little else than these two vocal but unintelligible presences downstairs.

So I brought over my wife. She pressed an ear humoringly to the floorboards, harked, pronounced the two of them father and grown son working puzzles in the paper, hand-minded folks finding holiday hours on the comics page.

MY WIFE once more: that little rizzle of hair on the upper spread of her foot, for one thing, and bullying breasts muted by a bra the color of those bandages you were expected to stretch resourcefully around a sprain.

She would take her dinner to the telephone table—a treacly salad, a clod or two of chocolate—and wipe the hair out of her eyes when it came time to play it down again that something was considered forgiven, if only in a newsy sort of way.

DOG AND OWNER

NOT TOO LONG after having insisted, when the day finally arrived, on being seated, by myself, at an arm's-length remove from tables now pushed together in makeshift, banquet-style annexation, and then (once the guests, the few of them there were, relations of hers, with a few drinks in them apiece, had at last taken their leave), having made short work of fussing myself free from whatever might have been "put sacred" between the two of us (because the girl and I had never been close: at most, I had seen to setting up, by her side and in my stead, in eulogy to some vague, perishing beauty of hers, an ornate and embellishable absence into which, from farther and farther off, I had been good about throwing even more endearments, encouragings, and so forth)—not too long afterward, in short, I remember having stopped one afternoon for an overpostponed lunch, something quick and unconsidered, in a bystreet coffee shop whose narrow band of windows, once I had got myself established at last in a booth, cropped the second, and terminal, stories of the buildings across the street in a way that gave a persuasive, even elegant, suggestion of a grand upsweep just out of view, as if the little I could make out were in fact foundationary of something vast and overtowering, an abrupt city impending over the low-strung town I was despised in. This last, of course, was exactly the sort of conviction I was getting much better at keeping propped up, sawhorse style, above the lurid floor of my forties; and thus, after the meal, chancing the streets again and resorting, almost at once, to the town's one catchy avenue, the line of buildings looking understandably stooped and unfinished to me now, I would halt every half-minute or thereabouts to tilt my head back in regard of, say, a storefront that shouldered a couple of floors of sooty apartments, and then, taking the full, unruly measure of what I saw, let my eyes step everything up to what, until now, had been merely implied heights. In no time, I was entertaining, banking on, similarly enlarging abstractions about people, persons—namely, that they no doubt had to be just getting started right there where their bodies stopped short, and that there were bound to be further, more considerable attractions just above eyeshot; and it was then that I noticed it, a figure hunching its way with unsteady gait toward me along the sidewalk, as if there were at least one extra foot to be worked into the problem of walking, and when this form drew close, I could make out an outnumbered-looking man of about my age, arms blundering outward, one hand busying itself with the ticky clickwork of a ballpoint, and a face devoted to an assailant nose and metrical eye-blinks—the eyes, it seemed, forever figuring their owner in and then out again of difficult, riskful head counts. There was such an aboveboard loveliness in the joinery of all parts of him, in the way his body seemed to verge away from itself and into the space upkept between the two of us, that I decided, at once, to make an experience of him, to call him up out of himself then and there, though it might well have been little more than tricks, hoaxes, of reposturing that I was capable of bringing off, and it is entirely likely that I had already dropped to my knees, and it could have been either one of us, in fact, who let out, "Not here, not here," for he was by now stretching an arm toward a car across the street, a four-door dejecture done over in a low-down, militarized olive-gray, and we went to the thing, and got in, and he took off in the direction of some watercourse or another, because it was a town dulled by water, streamy silences of it, fits and starts of a bigger, dishevelled river downstate; and letting him be keeper of the quiet, I threw my mouth open to the knowledges, the crammed expertise, I fell back on in just such sudden but slow-going crosstown companionships, remarking, to start, that there was a way to cough without even having to part the lips—the most it required was setting off a dampened clicking just behind the Adam's apple; and that at the baccalaureate shithouse that was still keeping me on, "with reservations," from month to month, I had helped myself to the discovery that if you were true to the same pair of trousers for four or five days running (here I pointed, by way of example, to the set of flagging flannels in which I had been carrying myself about), your faithfulness would make of the change collecting in the pockets (and here I gave some demonstrational tinklings) a weighty, wallet-rivalling wealth; and that it was not so much that the dog and its owner come to look like each other as that they both by degrees take on a trim, unbidden resemblance to a third party, a truant, dancing an unseen attendance on the two of them as it plunges its way forth to take at last the delayed, necessary spills.

The man's watch, I now noticed, as he ventured some even more finical turnings of the steering wheel, had not been strapped onto him so that the dial, the outcase, would face below the arm in the routine, oblivion-securing fashion of the desk-bound, but instead was posited at the outermost bend of the wrist, just beyond where the half-globelet of bone stuck out, and thus fronted away from him entirely, so that no carpal motion, or any greater chance mission of the arm itself, would ever risk bringing the dial into his view. For this, you see, was the weekend we gained an hour, and people, persons, were understandably slower, more bashful, in prying their way into further others, or running themselves on a bias through whoever else there was, or keeling forward into a chosen one, once and (let them hope) done.

But this man, perish the thought, was nobody of mine, though my fingers steal, stole, forever downward everywhere regardless.

They could make a day of it on anyone.

I REMEMBER coming to, much later, in a room, an uprooted-looking bedroom, where a woman was operating an opaque projector, one of those big-bulbed, plastic gimmicks, half toy, that gave off the private and chastening smell of clothes being ironed and that was throwing any chosen small objects onto the one undecorated wall at many times their meek, certain size. (This was a shovy, fast-swallowing woman with an unheated air of seniority about her and thick, lengthsome hair parted so severely, so opponentially, that it fell onto me in twinned antagonisms.) I know I sat up, at once, on the brink of the bed as her pinked fingers ushered things in and out of the display area of the projector (she had the thing propped up, you see, on her lap), and I remember her making a show of the discernibles, incommodities, released from the pockets of my pants: my keys, the mostly invalid few of them I had strung along the lower bend of a paper clip, the snaggled serrations of each now looking gouged out, geologic; the butt of a pencil I had once held dear; a little breaking, an abruption, of kitchen-floor linoleum I had taken to carrying about because there were gabbing faces and sheer, intentional geography discoverable within it once you got the knack of how such things demanded to be seen.

The man, of course, was still lying only several, witting inches away from me, compact and delicate in his sleep, packed into it, practically, and there was such a kindly deportment to him, and such a thrift in the inturning of his limbs, that I kept my voice down when the only thing for me to tell the woman, the one thing left to get rubbed in, was that I could remember having sought my father's counsel only once: I had needed some help with getting around the endearment called for in the salutation of a postcard I was destining for a friend, or for a stand-in for the friend I was impatient to have come forward, because this

was the summer between the grade when I last looked to people
for what they had already seen of everybody else, and the grade
when I started seeing that the people I looked at were blocking
my view of even fuller numbers of people behind them, that
people up close were in fact coming between me and the rest
of the world, that the most I might make out of the people on
the other side would be the perimetrical fraction of midriff that
now and then showed through when the person behind was a
hair broader than the person out front, or (just once) a pair of
arms spiring above a head in what might have been mere exercise but which in my eyes acquired the status of purposeful
beckoning; and the criticism thus set down now with greatest,
red-inked frequency on the backs of report cards was that my
voice no longer travelled direct to the teacher's face, but went
around the face, or to the side of it, and that my answers not only
were louder than what the acoustics of the classroom called for,
but seemed addressed to someone in back of the teacher, someone on the other side of the wall behind her, or somebody several rooms down. And thus the postcard—the front of the picture
postcard I was subjecting at last to reminiscence, the one I had
been intent on seeing off: the thing threw in your face, naturally,
the name of the beach town, the resort, spelled rollickily in hollowed block letters, every one of which gave out, windowlike, on
a different span of the same boardwalk, the plankway on which
I had to keep to my latecomer's place between my father's sog-
ging trunks and my mother's tagalong dress when, at mealtime,
my parents halted in front of one concession after another to
have a look at whoever had been at the meat, and what had been
made of it, how unproportioned or lonesome the sandwiches
looked once they had at last been let down onto the paper plates,
and my father or the other always saying, "We can do better," or
"The day is still young"; and on the matter, at last, of the salutation for my postcard, what my father therefore recommended
was *Buddy Walt*, but when my ballpoint got going between my
fingers, what I was writing was *Friend Walter* instead, and then I of

course crossed out *Walter*—more than crossed it out; overspread it with stickied opulences of the violet ink—and then got rid of *Friend*, put it out of my sight, cancelled it with even more busied stickiness, and, after many an airborne hesitation of the writing hand, I simply wrote *You!*—Y*O*U*!; i.e., Why, oh, you!—and left the address panel blank, spotless, unmolested, on the strength of the unforeseen conviction that like-natured postmen would certainly recognize virtues in the high points of my penmanship and keep the card in noticeable motion along the upper currents of the mailstream until the thing got itself claimed, finally, by anyone eyewatery and room-ridden enough to have expected delayed, devout word from somebody anyplace else.

For, you see (I told the woman), the actual writing of what I wrote on the postcard was brought to happen in a tent-trailer, a sulfur-yellow, boxlike concernment that had been hired only for the week, vacation week, and that was hitched to the car and had to be folded out at both ends to get the up-spreading canvas portioned into taut walls and a roof, and to produce the cantilevered ledges on which we piled the bedding and went through the hours of degraded nighttime that we had come to expect in place of sleep, my parents at one end, gone weak in their horse sense, and I at the other, still picky about my feelings, all boned up on myself, contesting my life—for the little I had set down in the message panel of the postcard could have been only the first of many reminders to stop siccing my heart on the locals and just get my loneliness finally right.

ALL TOLD

THE DAY MY SISTER DIED, I was the first to make a parting from the packs of shadow in the tall room. She did not exactly look hemmed in by death.

I still remember her telephone number. Something happens to a phone number when it is held too readily in recall. The movement of those digits through memory gains the unheaviness, the fated headway, of haiku. You feel foreordained in even your faintest of furies.

I mean, there was something physical about the way I kept ringing her up—a finger maybe in the ribs.

My parents later attracted a calamity of their own. Crossed the center line in their cozy sedan. (I was the one who had put them up to "seeing some lights.") I thus had an inherited house all to myself. But if I came around to learning that places can have consequences, too, I hardly mean only the easy contagions of furniture, or any room's inevitable, irreversible digestion of its contents. What I wish to insist is that anything you look at can have a way of holding itself against everything else. I thus became a specialist in the fevered and exactive marriage of a week to ten days. The women all had shrewd, fortunate hair.

But I can bring most of them back—my family, at the least.

I will forever be cueing them up in gesture, throes, locution.

My father: I can read a book as uncleanly as he could. I leave a luxuriant organicity to behold on most pages. Hardenings, cakings, fingertrails.

And my mother: I line my upper teeth behind the lowers until my jaw shoots forward a little and I am no longer speaking up for others.

But my sister! I cannot carry out her life with anything I am currently putting over on people.

Even in dirty weather, my hands are tied.

THE SUMMER I COULD WALK AGAIN

THEY ARE NEVER in the house at the same time.

My cousin's skin isn't packed on right. It bunches up at the knees. When she talks, she hoops a bracelet back and forth along her arm from the wrist all the way to the elbow – that's how thin.

She's low on people and places, you can tell.

She knows better than to call me the man of the house.

She says a new day is too big a thing right away. You have to nap it down until you fit inside.

She's allowed in my bed. Her snores come in long lines that tip way up at the end. What I hear is questions – somebody asking me the same thing over and over, something simple.

My answer is no.

I place my leg over hers, then hers over mine. Her limp hand goes anywhere I decide. I uncurl her fingers and put them over where I am all wrong. I'm allowed in her purse. The mirror inside her compact holds exactly my face.

"Did you sleep?" she says afterward.

THERE ARE TWO of them next door, brothers, a year or so apart. Their names would just ruin everything. I loop electrical wire around my wrist, pale my neck and arms with talcum. I let them practice on me one at a time.

First it counted only if I could get them to keep their eyes open. Then it counted either way.

Today it's the younger.

My hand on his arm, the promised rise of bicep.

WE SIT ON OUR HANDS and our feet. Different parts of us go to sleep at different times. Nothing gets put away.

There is a list, my cousin says, of everything my mother knows is not right. I cannot get her to show it to me or even tell me what room it might be in.

"It is all written down about you," she says.

"YOUR MOTHER works where?" my cousin says.

"For the state."

"Only time anybody ever tells me that is when they work in a liquor store."

LEAVING, she says, "Is everything off that gets taken off?"

She looks me over for signs.

"YOU DON'T KNOW the first thing about it," my cousin says.

I tell her about the brothers.

"Besides those," she says.

She takes my fingers in hers and puts the two of us into where she is nothing but mush and pulp.

"You're one hole short," she says.

THEY COME OUT of the water, new hair staining their shins. To get them into the house, I tell them I can give birth.

They follow me up the stairs and into the bathroom. I am good at pulling down my pants. I sit on the toilet and squeeze and squeeze until I get something finally sizable to come out.

It's the only reason I eat—to get off the seat and point down into the bowl at what should be the beginning of arms or a heart.

THE BEST WAY to clean a carpet in the long run, she says, is to pick everything out of it by hand. I'm on my knees, going from room to room, filling my pail with fuzzballs, bits of paper, pebbles, shells of beetles. Every room has something different for her to flop on.

"One summer, I was like that with girls," she says. "Every ponytailed little brat up and down the block thought she had me spoken for."

She comes from a family big enough, she says, for everyone in it to have always been looking the other way. According to her, this is what makes her an only child.

"IT'S NOT A MOUTH," she says. "I already have a mouth."

I am folding the big towels.

IT IS LONG AFTER dark when I knock on the screen door.

The younger one comes toward me through the kitchen, his eyes and mouth shadowed off, his face just a blacked circle.

I know him by height.

"We're not allowed out, and you're not allowed in," he says.

I look down at my clean feet.

IS IT ONE mistake after another, or is it the same one divvied up to make it last from one day to the next?

The door to my mother's room is always shut but never locked. Her life is private but not secret. I have to remember which way the hooks of her clothes hangers point before I take anything off them. My body has no smell of its own yet. Nothing remains of me on whatever I put myself against.

Nothing settles on me, either.

That's the thing.

Nothing ever comes to any kind of rest.

I AM STANDING along the road when a car comes close, slows.

"Are you selling something?" a voice says.

There is a man and a woman in the car, a couple.

"Don't anybody sell anything anymore along this road?" the man says. "This looks like the road."

"She's not looking at us," the woman says.

"It don't look like it," the man says.

"Maybe she's not selling something right this very minute but has plans for the future," the man says. "That could be it. How about we drive around some more and come back in maybe half an hour and then see if she's gotten a head for business?"

I run back to the porch, where my cousin has the carrots ready for me to peel.

"Who was that?" she says.

"Somebody looking for Dad."

I GET INTO their room just once. I ask which dresser drawers I am allowed to open.

It's not a dresser, they tell me. It's a chest of drawers.

They are ready for bed.

MY COUSIN no longer gives out information, because of things I do with it.

She tells me about where she came from originally. At one time it was the seat of something, she says. The world wore itself onto the people who lived there and onto the legs of the pants and the sleeves of the shirts and the raincoats that the people put themselves through to get out of its way. When they undressed at night, the clothes fell onto the floor along the track the world had taken.

Otherwise, she says, nobody slept.

THE DOCTOR TELLS my mother to stay off her feet for a week.

"You have the air blowing right over you," she says.

I get up and turn things off.

MY READING matter is the warnings on the backs of cleaning products. I have the bottles lined up on the bathroom floor. The stickers come right out and say Do Not.

My mother is downstairs making the sandwiches the way she was taught. My cousin's are just stacks of sliced bread, nothing in between unless she's in a mood.

I come down in my underwear.

"Is it doing you any good?" my mother says. "Does she go over things with you? Is anything coming across? Does it pay me to keep her? Is she ever on time? What does she do around here all day? Do you listen to a thing she says?"

I HAVE BEEN TOLD that when people say they see my father in me, I am to do one of two things.

The first is just to tell them that it must be only because he's trying to get their attention because he wants something again. Otherwise he wouldn't be showing himself in me of all people.

The other is for when people have already stayed too long. I'm supposed to say, "Where? Point him out. Show me where, so I can pull him out all the way. Maybe I can shit him out. Think that would work? Let's go see."

I have done both, but sometimes I just picture my body glassed over and my father motioning from within, bobbing up now and then between my bones, no big trouble.

MY MOTHER is back at work.

"I took some things of mine to a dry cleaner once, as a treat," my cousin says. "The man behind the counter looked everything over and said, 'Who wore these?'"

I'M IN THE GRASS when they come up from behind. One grabs me by the ankles, the other under the arms. I like them this quiet. They carry me across the field – the sky is bowled above me – and drop me into the stream.

The water is cold but not deep.

They run off, leaving me staring up.

Then I'm on the warm macadam. One has my shirt and shorts and is riding his bike in a circle, whipping them dry.

I am in his.

Everything sticks.

"You're the instigator," the other says.

WHO CAN SLEEP? There was a penlight flashlight on a beaded chain my grandmother bought me once. I had to keep clicking it on and off and on again to make sure the thing still worked. It finally no longer did. It was a relief to go on to something else.

In like manner, I count on losing the use of my eyes because of what I do with them—closing and opening them too many times, expecting fresh letdowns in the way things look from one instant to the next.

I'M UPSTAIRS in the bathroom, hearing everything.

"Are you the mother?" It's a woman's voice.

"I'm who the mother pays," my cousin's voice says.

"What about the boy—he's here?"

"Can't say. I might've dozed off."

"He was obviously here earlier. I understand he had some company."

"He's in and out."

"Tell him the mother of the boys next door wants him to know he's made two very nice boys very sick to their hearts."

"Count on it."

I'm on the bowl with my legs tighter together, not ready to see what else might have happened since I last had a look down, when I first saw toes on a foot, a definite mouth.

FEMME

I USED TO VISIT a younger man in the big, voluminal city, the one that maddened itself out between twin rivers. He would call and say, "Just get here." I would drive half a day to a town within two hours of the place, then park, and ride a bus the rest of the way. There would be the rummaged abundance of his hair, the blooded trouble of his eyes, hands runted becomingly—but he always just wanted me to go out with him with his friends, a characterful alumni brigade. Once, one of them had found the "perfect winter bar," and it was in fact winter, forced-air heat had dried up all their faces, and my younger man returned from the barkeep with some timely femme sparkle for me to spurn through a straw, unobscured spirits for himself. Our table was two tables brought together unlevelly. His friends were lounging quietly in whichever private, humble injuries could have then been current.

But my love for him must have been flush with the line of his arm as often as he got it propped up to make his point: that things should be kept figmentary on people, between people—

So I suppose, yes, we were serious about each other, only graver than two men usually are about failings they are fleeing.

Later, in his apartment, a walk-up, I watched him beat himself back from me again.

BEFORE HIM, I had had a wife: a wife, true, who kept a glaze over everything. I would have to scratch my way through it if I hoped to find anything unhypothetical. (She exhausted her hair with denigratory tints, and there was a stirless dark to her eyes. Contact was chancy, ungladdening.) It was a period, understand, of rationed, grating embraces, and then one day she came out with a baby, sprang it on me in a bassinet upstairs. I know I must have eventually confused the thing with mock holidays, and lonely toilet drills, and homemade cereals that just sank in the milk, and I know I must have stood the kid up in front of uncles and ball-rolling aunts, and then she vanished with it into her vague-faced, waiting family. These were people who uprooted themselves tooth and nail, hurried their furniture over highways into ditchy, isolating towns. They were letter writers, but they mostly just wrote, "We know about you."

I HAVE SINCE turned many a corner in what I know of myself.

I can take apart a marriage, and sense when a possessiveness might be difficult to undo.

One morning I found a pill outside a neighbor's door. It was reason enough to have stooped some more. This was a vagrant, gray prescriptional with narrow characters sunken dingily into the face. I went back to my place and gave the thing a concerned chew, then put my system on alert for any improving diddling within. I waited half an hour, an hour, an hour and a half.

I was living in an apartment complex. There is no use in hearing the term "apartment complex" unless it is taken immediately to mean a syndrome, a fiesta of symptoms.

On the other side of my bathroom, someone was living a life that called for lots of water. I would almost always hear it streaming remedially into the tub, the sink.

People, co-workers, naturally inquired about whether I had a girlfriend, and if I mentioned somebody "now gone from this world," I did so in the expectancy that by "this world" they would understand me to have meant not the entire subcelestial estate or national agitation, but just my unlargening residential snatch of it and the few places I might have once taken someone – the second-hand-clothing stores and bested restaurants of the unample town.

This town, you had to get your hands on a different, specialized map just to see it.

It was a hollowed-out dot of round-shouldered population. Roughnecks ran the college.

MY YOUNGER MAN: he had moved around a lot on people. A lot of casework, social work, had gone into him. He lived on purified tap water and spangled baked goods. His face rarely carried an expression to term, but there was expression in his elbow, a mien to be made out in either of the underarms.

Some nights it was all I could do to keep from adding my lips to the mouth of a bottle he had once put his mouth around when pausing for effect in some gracing self-criticism.

His face? He called it a rat face.

His ass? He said there was a word in his grandmother's tongue for the way the flab seemed to be coming up from it in little bubbles. It was a pimpling or a pilling my dabbling eye had never minded.

There was a bar of soap he had used a couple of times, a woman's soap, with womanly incurvature. I had held on to it. I would draw it unwetted along my cheek, the distance of my arm. I would try to bring a little back, however much of him might still be sticking to the thing, because I understood the molecules of soap to be especially grasping and retentive, and the skin of a man to be not all that loyal to the body.

WHEN YOU live in apartments, understand, you go over the communal walls daily, fingering for sightways, cracks, exposures, scopes.

You resort further and further to the TV, just to hear voices coming physically out of pictured people and not through ceilings, cupboardry, the floor.

I was no model rider of the bus, either. I saw arms, swaying legs, that might have belonged on anyone. Everybody was the same body, no matter the twists of personality, the agonied differences of fit and build.

Then I must have been caused to fall for a woman, a regular on the jumbly, crosstown run, because one day one part of her would be arisen, pivotal, summonsy, awag—a chancing hand, perhaps, or gleamed, unsecretful ankle. By the next day, the center of her would have shifted. A couple of public weeks like this, and finally she said, "So what do you think? Could you use a friend?"

I moved my things in. This woman turned out to have a daughter, a struggler, who was late to take after her. The girl's body was now in brutal pursuit of the mother's. The girl seized the mother's most liable features, and brought them—panging, pushful—to semblant possession on herself.

The mother's face gave ground. I watched it unpile itself.

Her voice was a gurge.

I would tread tenorlessly on floorboards on my way to the stairs.

Our life thereafter was jumpy and bare.

THE BOY

T HE BOY was raised in a city that had the look and feel of a
state capital but in fact was not even a county seat. The buildings—big, brutish granite piles—gave everybody the wrong idea.
Travellers would see the castellated skyline from the highway,
sheer off at the exit, park their cars, then climb steep steps to what
they hoped, despite the absence of signs, of plaques, would prove
to be a mint, a museum, a monument. Once inside, they would
find themselves in cramped, fusty living quarters. Somebody—an
old woman in a housecoat or a bed jacket—would look up from
a sofa and say, "Let a person sleep." The boy, on the other hand, did
not have the look and feel of anything big or promising. You
couldn't look up his name in books. Even as a child, he had always
remained many removes from himself. Wherever he stood—near
the swing set on a playground, say—he was never inarguably there,
but his absence was always firsthand. His absence, in fact, was so
commanding, so convincing, that people around him were often
confused about just exactly where they too now stood. Obviously,
his parents must have caught on very early to the unexampled
form of ventriloquism the boy had evolved, a ventriloquism that
entailed displacing not just his voice but his entire flute-thin
body, and they made the necessary adjustments—sudden half-

steps or about-faces—in their own strides. That's why people thought they walked funny, that's why people thought they looked funny together as a family.

ONE DAY, well gone in childhood, the boy sat at the kitchen table and watched the father solder together two wires on the boy's tape recorder.

The tape recorder was of the old, reel-to-reel type.

The father was not especially good with his hands. In fact, the soldering iron—the risk that its use introduced into his life—was a terror. More important, the father was unforgiving. He was so unforgiving that he gave in, time after time, doing everything for the boy out of a big, banging spite. With every splenetic dab of the soldering iron, the father thought he was defecting from a deductive scheme that always runs: Father, Mother, Son.

The boy was convinced that by destroying his playthings he was accomplishing something similar.

WALKING HOME from the high school he attended at the other end of the city, the boy would often linger in a park near the very tallest of the buildings. Crestfallen tourists would on occasion approach him. Once, a long-throated, heavily talcumed woman asked, "Have you a pen on your person?" The boy slued around slowly and exaggeratedly, as if to see whether there was a third party involved, an attendant bearing supplies. There was only his own angled, outbound body and, at a respectable distance, her own, the globulet of a tear glissading down her cheek. The woman moved on. There were plenty of men in the park whose pockets were full of pens and whatever else there might be a call for.

ONE DAY early in his eleventh-grade year, the boy was summoned from his social-studies class to the office of the guidance counselor. The guidance counselor was a short-winded block of a man with corned teeth and an overexerted vocabulary. He explained that to the best of his knowledge it would be in the best interest of both the boy and the school if, for the remainder of his tuition, he were enrolled as a girl. He explained that the parents had already been informed and that the papers had already been drawn up and dispatched for them to sign. That night, the boy's mother took the boy shopping for the pair of Mary Janes, the jumper, enough white blouses for a week. The boy became very popular at school, excelled at all his subjects to the extent that was then expected of girls, and enjoyed many boyfriends and admirers, all of whom he did his very best to delight. At the commencement ceremony, the guidance counselor delivered a long speech about the boy and his progress. The speech was full of words like "miracle" and "rapture" and "angel." During the peroration, the guidance counselor publicly proposed to the boy. They were married a week afterward in an elaborate but rushed ceremony, during which the minister looked content in the knowledge that this smell would cover up that smell and so forth down the line, domino-style. Two weeks later, the guidance counselor died loudly and tumultuously in his sleep. The boy slipped out of his negligee and slumped across the dark city to the house of his parents.

WITH HIS DIPLOMA and a cajoling, loopily handwritten letter of application, the boy was offered employment three hundred and forty-two miles to the right of his bed if he was facing the wall that held the window, a position he favored. He engaged a room, sight unseen, over the telephone.

A week before the boy was to depart, his mother decided he would need a rug. She drove him to a carpet store to have a look at remnants.

The boy watched the salesman slide a licorice cough drop into his mouth from the box in the pocket of his shirt.

"You certainly know your way around in here," the salesman said eventually to the boy.

The boy turned away and paged through some carpet samples bound together in a thick, shaggy book.

"I was saying, ma'am, that your son here has sure been spending a lot of time in this store," the salesman said.

"We'll want something for the floor," the mother said.

"Okay," the salesman said. "What are we talking about?"

"It's just one big room," the mother said.

"How big of a room?" the salesman said.

The mother looked at her son. "How big a room?"

The boy did not answer.

"It's one state over," the mother said.

THERE IS an explanation for patricide that works in every case. In every case, there is a soda machine close at hand.

The boy was always thirsty. The boy was always hurrying across the street to the machine, buying one can at a time, carrying it back to his room to drink at the table. The father was in town only for a visit. The greasy whorls of the father's thumbprints had already blurred the cover of the hobby magazine the boy had bought for the father to leaf through. Also on the table was an iron that the boy worried was prowing in a different direction every time he returned from the machine.

"You drink way too much soda," the father said, finally.

"I'm thirsty," the boy said.

"Then drink water."

"I hate water."

"Soda don't even quench your thirst. Look at the money you're throwing away."

"If it doesn't quench my thirst, then tell me what it does do."

"It makes the inside of your mouth and throat nice and cold for a couple seconds. That's it. Water would do just as good."

The boy and the father sat and wordlessly pushed their points.

The knife presented itself to the boy as if in shimmery italics. The boy could not remember ever having bought the thing. It was a heftless, nervous-atomed, self-disowning simulacrum of what a knife was supposed to look like in such a low-built town.

As on so many occasions, this was the boy's first time, but everything rang a bell—a cracked, mootish, spanging bell. Each clank of it brought him a clangorous bit closer to the understood you.

THIS IS NICE OF YOU

I WAS A MAN dropping already well through my forties, filthy
with myself, when, taking a turn at the toilets one afternoon,
I met two brothers—they said they were brothers—who swore
they had a sister, a schoolteacher, an officer of instruction at the
county college, a whirlwind midlife turmoil of everything already put to ruin, who had gone off from a new marriage in an
old car, an upkept and ennobling sedan, but had returned now
to the apartment and was living there alone with the little runoff
there was from the marriage—some outcurved appliances, apparently, and low-posted furniture promoting its own mystery but
becoming figurable in certain concentrations of TV light—and,
above all, a telephone (on a pedestal, they insisted), the hand-
piece of which she gripped in lieu of exercise, or in fury, and I
thus let out my little, reliable cry that I was in fact a student of
the telephone, that it was a debasing apparatus in the main, with
its meager economy of bells and tones, and the intimacy of the
mouthpiece that sent your breath, tiny aftervapors of it, back
toward your lips, so that regardless of the party accepting the
outgoing products of your voice, you were, at most, in a further,
rivalling exchange with yourself alone, and this is what must
have brought the two of them around, the men who proclaimed

brotherhood with the woman, because they offered me her phone number, put it at my disposal on a piece of paper one of them had already committed it to, a snipping from a menu, and the looks the men were now giving me had deletions in them, already, of my exact, beanpole shape and size. So off I went to a pay phone, the nearest canopied one I could find. The woman answered after the second ring and said she needed a lift right that very moment into the little, unlevel city close by.

She was idling in the doorway of the building when I pulled up in front, and I helped her into the car, then got back in myself. I had always had a way of not having to look at people that nonetheless brought them to me in full, and so I still am certain of the susceptive and impressible complexion, the shimmer on the mouth, a lipstick of low brilliance, a difficulty around the eyes, the hair short and rayed out exclamationally, skin bagged up over the elbow bone, conflict even in how her arms stayed at her sides — in sum, a spinal loveliness for me, an off-blonde quantity with shadowed, thumbworn hollows that put me out of as much as I might have ever known of women before.

I set the two of us into the narrow traffic, and I remember telling her, by way of explaining the little burden which I had shifted, by now, from the shelf of the dashboard and onto my lap, that when you lived as I then did, a daily newspaper came to count for a lot, although instead of the thick-supplemented local paper, I bought a trimmer one from a backlying town — not, of course, for any affluences of native data it carried, but as an article of houseware: a rough immaculacy in four lank sections, a set of fresh, hygienic surfaces to come between the table, say, and whatever I had going for me on the table, if the table was where I was going forward — because what else so cheap comes so clean and far-spreading?

The woman told me that her own trouble with paper was that through a modest hole, no larger than a quarter, that had been drilled a foot or so above the floor (the standard height, she had reasoned, of legitimate electrical outlets), and by means of which her faculty office had at last gained communication with the roomier but unoccupied office next door, she more and more often shot a single sheet of paper, plain copier paper she had rolled just barely into a tube, so that after landing on the floor of the neighboring office the paper would preserve little if any of the curl, and there would be nothing written or typed on it, of course, and it was always a blank sheet that had been ageing on her desk for some time and had already been moved around, or advanced, from station to station on the desktop, coming into further creaselets and crimps and other infirmities – paper, in short, still too bare and unfraught to be thrown responsibly and forgettably away, and yet too seasoned and beset with irritations of the surface (a molelike blemish, say, or what looked like a tiny hair, an eyelash, sunk into it, or frecklings, or notational pressings of a fingernail), too wrought, in sum, for the paper to be appointed to any secure curricular purpose. Her office, she claimed, was in fact full of such paper, much-handled and singularized sheets of it by the loose, functionless hundred.

I had to get it across to the woman that I myself no longer had an office, or any other place to divide me reliably from everybody else, and that for much of the daylight I thus appeared to be among people because I kept putting myself where people came together into even closer-fitting assortments, the viewing areas and showrooms and rotundas and such: I took in the lean-to look of the women, the tongues coming and going in what the men kept thinking of to say – whole families of low knees for me to bark my shins against during the crowded and involving way out. At home afterward, in the one room where my life was packed down, I would keep my nose stuck in the safehold of the phone book, where the names of people suffered reduction to mere episodes of the alphabet and underwent humbling declensions down every column (Lail, Lain, Laine, Lainerd), and the names of streets, of the towns and townships, got docked in crude, heedless abbreviations (the vowels almost always the first to get poked out), and I would run my eyes over the telephone numbers themselves, each sequence of digits another fallible run of the infinite. I thus corrected my feelings for people and assembled myself emotionally into whatever else I had at hand–the obligating arms of the clothes hangers, usually, or the keen-angled understructure, the guardian legginess, of the ironing board.

The woman said that in her case, though, it was more a matter of making slow circuits of the classroom where she had to put across the Emporial Sciences, retail theory and methods, to heat-giving and suggestive young women, some of them world cruelties already. There was the cooing of empty stomachs in the hour just before lunch, and the braying and fizzle of loaded stomachs in the low hours of the afternoon. She would recite her notes in a voice barely loyal to any one octave, a tiny alluvium of slaver hardening at the corners of her mouth on the days she gave the glassy lozenges a slow, warming suck, and she would take lowering notice of how whatever she said succumbed at once to freak spellings and razzing paraphrase in the big, dividered notebooks; and because in midafternoon light the world looked as thorough, as filled in, as it was ever going to get, a better way to set about ruining her eyes was to review how hair had established itself on the arms of the young women, because almost every arm had brought across itself a welcome and diversifying shadow. On one girl it would be a fine, driftless haze afloat above the white of the arm, never seeming to touch down on the skin itself. (An atmosphere, at most, of Brazil-nut brown.) On another, it was as if copper wire, the narrowmost lengthlets of it, had been stuck into the fleshy batter of the thick, freckled forearms. On a third: a field of it–wheat-colored, thin-spun. On a fourth: a differencing, darkish updrift that shaded off as it approached the inner bend of the elbow, then re-emerged at the base of the upper arm as whiskery fringe. On others it was a brassy or rust-colored frizz, or it was as coarse as corn silk, or it looked fussed on, as if the arm had been slowly stroked with charcoal.

But here the woman broke off, or I may well have made an interruption of my own–I think I must have asked whether she was hungry, and she said if I was, and so on one of the lesser streets I parked the car and led her down into a belowstairs eating house I still remembered. Sandwiches were presently lowered in front of us. I watched her remove the festooned toothpick from hers and then play her fingers over the toasted planes before she took a fond, first bite.

"This is nice of you," she said.

I must have looked at her in the way I then had of getting people to speak so they would not seem to be dwelling any longer on my features, because if on the well-set face the mouth and eyes are said to seem frozen in elegant orbit about the tip of the nose, then mine was a face that beholders, regarders, could not help trying to round off with greater success, to goad the particulars of it back into the arcs they had wandered away from—the mouth, for instance, having been pursed and pinched suchwise that it seemed resident more on one side of the face than the other—and there were other signs of original strife to be busied with (slapdash eyebrows unbunched, it appeared, from reserves of hair elsewhere on my person; a showing of adult acne, a shrivelly little relevance of it, confined to the declivity of my nose); and so to be polite, the woman thus sank her gaze into her sandwich, and told me, in a voice lowered accordingly, that, one late-childhood summer, she had devoted herself to collecting postage stamps: it was a tongue-involving sideline to early-arriving puberty, and she liked having to lick the pale, gummed hinges instead of the sticky backs of the stamps themselves before entering everything into the hosting album; and once, during some foul weather between her and a brother (the older, thrown-over one, who had already made a habit of fooling the underside of his arm across the top of hers and calling her "pussified"), she reached for the shoe box in which she had let duplicate stamps accumulate—Spanish ones, mostly, of a fading orange—and sent the box slooshing through the lower air so that the stamps showered onto the brother's bare legs with a full, delicate harm.

The woman was now touching up the surface of her iced tea with tiny activities, initiatives, of the longspun spoon. I myself was good at getting my touch onto things, although in a way that seemed to mix up the motive atoms inside them, but I was satisfied that for the moment my sandwich, the unbitten-at half of it, was still displayable and stable and local to my plate.

The woman went on to say that, as a child, she had been bundled off, many an afternoon, to the slope-ceilinged quarters of a bachelor uncle, who, when speaking of anybody not immediately present, could not bring himself to use the person's name but instead would say "an acquaintance of mine in..." and then mention the name of some lapsed homeland, or little-loved rural orchestra, or backset building about to come down; and it was never a riddle, this device of his (not once could the girl have been expected to identify any of the subjects), and no matter how often and aloud he insisted that particularizing persons any further—bringing even a first name down upon any one of them—would have been indecent, he claimed, much like doing things to people while they slept, the girl accepted all of the uncle's prim and extravagant evasion for what he surely must have intended it to be: a neat, protective trick to space the world out a little further in her favor, to scatter the population so that wherever her hand might at last come down, it would have to be on herself alone.

And here I could sense that the woman wanted from my mouth an account of as much as I myself might have ever managed of attachment, so I told her I had once owned a house (a rising, really, of much-fingered, handwrought architecture that amounted to a little family of rooms above garages: a boxlike building with a rattly thorax of downspouts and drainpipes and an unfolded but full-toned fire escape), and I had had for a time a boarder, a student, a high-colored, loose-packed representative of declining girlhood, hung with necklaces and barrettes, a girl of precise but shifting leanings and inclinations; and the afternoon she had come around to ask after the room, I stood in the entranceway, handshaken and asweat, and from what would later be my memory of the girl, I made off with, first, how every pore of her nose seemed to be sheltering within itself a tiny dark seed-let, a grain of something immediately, enormously valuable. And an almost lipless mouth (just a slit, practically), the teeth inside looking wet, watered—it was my life's chore, at that instant, to keep from sending the back of my thumb blotterlike across the line of them (I was later to learn she drank everything cold and through the narrowest of straws). And her hair: it was tea-col-ored hair she had, long and reachful, an unstopped downcome of it. Tall for a girl, but she managed to stay out of much of her height and put herself across as somebody backward, or behind.

I must have told the girl, as best I could, that I of course had a wife, a full-faced, imperishable partner, though for the moment she was gone otherwhere in the marriage, and here the woman, my present companion, my tablemate, whose feet were now parked, in parallel, on the grade of my upper leg, interrupted to say that her husband, too, had been such a liar, and what could I bring up by way of reply other than that a lie is a truth struck through with other, further truth, or that a lie is the present multiplied by the past, or that a lie is an outcry of borrowed hope? The woman gave me an allowed look of disgust, her eyes lowered but still popular with me, and on I went with what had now become the girl of my story.

For there had been a great, gainful carpet in the room I put the girl into, a matty expanse of coarse, grabby piles, an engrossing affair that took things into itself and held them tight, misered them, and I of course insisted that the girl not bother herself with its upkeep, that I enjoyed weekly access to a prestigious, upstanding vacuum cleaner; but no sooner was the girl out of the house each morning than I would withdraw from my room, where time was unportionable, and loose myself into the tick-tock impertinence of the girl's room and get down on my knees, and, going after the carpet first with my fingers, then with a forceps, and finally by unspooling lengths of clear package-sealing tape and pressing them against the tufts in neat rectangles to catch what I might have missed, I brought vast tracts of the carpet to depletion, recovering not simply the girlinesses, the girleries, one would expect (buttons, straight pins, downed jewelry), but flirtier personalia in the form, say, of a stray confetto brought into the world when a page had been wrung without caution from a spiral-bound notebook, or some pleated paper shells of the chocolates she required, or one of the bargain antihistamines she took to get her naps going, or a trash-bag tie ragged enough to show the kinked line of the wire within (this I would get wound around my finger), or a cough drop enwrapped like a bonbon (I would undo the wings of the wrapper and have to decide whether to suck the drop all down or begin chewing it midway) – I became the following, the public, that these things, these off-fallings, had come to have; but mostly there was hair, afloat above the uppermost pushings of the fabric of the carpet an almost continuous haziness of loose hairs of all lengths and sources, and I would have to set them out on a fresh sheet of paper and assort them according to the regions of the body they had taken their departure from, and in no time I had nestlike filiations of broken filaments and smaller involvements of the hairs that made me think of hooks, of barbs, of treble clefs, and each pile required a separate envelope, to be filed in a separate shoe box for every sector of the body until, I hoped, the boxes themselves would no longer be enough and I would have raised something semblable, brought up something equal in volume to the comprehensive girl herself.

And her wastebasket! For every bit of rubbish, every dreariment she tossed into the thing, I would, in secret, deposit a reciprocal discard of my own, matching a spotted, confessory tissue of hers with a lurid throwaway after my own heart – the cardboard substructions of a fresh parcel of underwear, maybe, or tearings from pantyhose I now and again pressed against a span of my forearm to work onto it the complications of female shading I otherwise made do, choosily, without.

I thus built the two of us up together in her trash!

One afternoon—it was another of those unsampled days when the world humors us each a little differently to keep us nicely on our last legs—I discovered in the wastebasket an inch-deep text-book of hers, a paperback with a celery-colored cover that had come partly unglued, and this dilapidation I paired off, naturally, with a name-your-baby guide to whose pages, during my recur-rent turnings of them, in bed or at table, I had contributed dried produces of my person, a chemical splendor entirely mine. This coupling sent a sudden spigoty thrill from me that forced an un-buckling and an unzipping and a cleanup with a handkerchief I then ventured responsively into the wastebasket as well.

It was in the bathroom afterward that I found a suds-clouded puddle on the unlevel floor of the tub, a little undrained remain-der, rimmed with offscum, of the girl's prolonged early-morn-ing soak, and this was as much as I needed to get on my hands; I pressed them flat against the wet porcelain, then flapped them around in the air, and that was when I noticed it—in the amphi-theater of the toilet bowl, an orange-yellow tint, or value, to the waters.

When the girl arrived home that evening, I told her, of course, that I had discovered fresh, unforeseen trouble within the tank of the toilet (a misalignment of the trip lever, a waywardness of the float ball, a misarticulation of the lift wires, kinks and defects, really, throughout the entire system) and that, in fine, it was a con-traption now operable only by means of advanced and strenuous equilibrial manipulations that it would be unseemly, inhospitable, of me to presume to burden her with—so that from here on out, following any leak or evacuation she need merely lower the lid and then, before quitting the room, ring the handbell that had been placed on the sink; I would see to everything else.

But the bell never rang, not even once, and from my window the next morning I watched the girl carry from the house a little plastic bag distended balloonishly, much like those bags you will remember having seen in the hands of children bearing homeward their solitary, carnival-prize goldfish. In fact, I never ran across the likes of the girl again. The man who came to collect her things — not the father, apparently, but an advocate, an upholder — I found to be dull-eared and lax in his speech, and the better part of his face seemed to have already begun making tiny, rotational departures from whatever it was that the eyes, themselves impressively mobile, were just that moment having to take in. (Was there a lamp in the house that was not that night slopping its wattage over everything?) I guess I was waiting for the man to take a laggard, last-minute interest in me, and by now I was pushing everything out into the paired first-person — it was, I said, "Our night shot," and I began including the two of us in whatever it might be doing out, the expected sprinkles and such — but he was no friendship buff, and he paid no heed to my telling him that the only dress of hers I had ever scrunged myself into even part of the way had been the simplest of them all, a large-buttoned wonder of depthless blue, and then only on the principle that one naturally fits whatever one has into whatever somebody else had first, or how else would the world keep getting any fuller with people? The man just went about the removal of the girl's things without having to be reminded too noticeably, I guess, of how every dick hangs by a thread.

My listener, though, had by this time brought about some becoming slowings of her arm — it was an arm inclinable to languorous diagonals and magicianly swoops through the air above the tabletop — but it no longer was involving itself with her plate, so I suggested we shove off, I made payment for the food, and on our way to the car, and then in the car as I took to following her pointings, the directional tilts of her head, she said that you naturally kept putting more and more of yourself into another person, at first wondering how much she can take, how much of you is accumulable and how much she can hold, and you're letting things out, disbursing yourself, and you've soon got things set up in her, and room is being made for even more of you, and if you bring this off with enough people, even two or three, what

you've got is at first a comfort, because you can pass yourself
along and move a little more widely through the world and leave
it to these others to man your grievances, your disappointments;
and what brought this to mind, the woman said, was a term of
financial hardship she had contrived for herself a few years back,
an unpaid leave of absence from scrupling letter grades onto
quiz papers (propped-up As, and upended Bs made to look, rather,
like fannies; all As and Bs, no Cs or anything lower, the difference between an A and a B having less to do with the accuracy
of whatever facts might have been impounded in the space the
woman had provided for an answer than with anything recall-
able about the way the enrollee had conformed her body to the
confining perpendiculars of her chair and the navel-level writing surface that projected from it, or the way there might one
day have been an unignorable blush on the instep of a once-mo-
seying foot, disburdened of its shoe, that had got itself trapped
in the grillwork of that cagelike involvement, intended for books,
that was welded to, or otherwise schemed into, the underworks
of the chair) – this had been a duration, in short, of controlled
difficulty, when the misexpenditure of even a twenty-dollar bill
had set her thrilling, gloating, over everything she would miss
out on, and one afternoon she had made an engagement for a
haircut, just a trim, and very early in the session the haircutter, a
woman poorly defined in the face but otherwise full of conspi-
cuities of emotion, set down the prevailing scissors and pressed
the flat of a lukewarm hand against the woman's cheek, held it
there for a good minute or longer, while the other hand eventually found its way into a drawer, a shallow treasury of slender
specialty scissors, one pair of which the cutter withdrew and
began routing deductively through the woman's hair, the other
hand staying put on the cheek, longer and longer, and the woman went home and for weeks afterward the bathtub was now a
more likely destination than any of the upright furniture, and it
got easier to fill the tub with further clarifying volumes than to
clear space on the difficult heights of the sofa, and she was hardly

claiming to have become a cleaner person in result – she in fact would often discover, voyaging about her body, a browned, fractionary detail of a larger crepe of toilet tissue that must have got itself stuck in some assy crevice and was impossible to get plucked out of the revolving suds – she was saying only that she spent more and more of her time thus immersed, ill off in water, and the haircutter had surely had a hand in it, the woman was doing some of the cutter's life now, coming into some of its wrong, because you sometimes have to look to somebody else's life to get the dimensions set back even part of the way around your own, and it should not have to be any less your own life when it comes from somebody else, and you could surely fudge a society out of any one available person and get this person doubling for the many, so that in the little run of things perpetuable from one person to the next, every loose moment stood to become a complete, active ultimacy.

But by now this was a new day, with only an hour or so off it already, and the place the woman had made me bring us to, the man's place, with a promise that the man was elsewhere – this was on a little offshoot of a street, a stewy efficiency apartment the color had long ago gone out of; and when, once in bed, still clothed, I found among the sheets and blankets a spoiling pair of the man's underpants, one of the leg openings of which was puckered into an avid, sloppy mouth, I held myself accountable for redisposing the fabric until I got a befitting featurelessness back onto it; but all the while, I am sure I had to make myself go over again in my mind that if the body is the porter of as many organs of affection as there might one day turn out to be, then the idea was to let the thing carry you to where you would otherwise never have any reason to arrive, because I listened for the unmelodious downslide of the woman's zipper, and then the woman made me put myself out of my own clothes, the attritional corduroys and overshirt, and got herself up at last onto the topic not of the man whose apartment this was (because his story was scarcely the story of how the boy who decides he is half a girl no sooner starts to worry about where the other half might be than he gets careless with where he rests his eyes, or what he gives even the feeblest of fingerholds to, and anything, even a crumbly triangle of pie offered on a saucer instead of on a pie plate proper, comes in easy, ready, wronging answer), but of her husband, and how, no more than a couple of months into the marriage, he had begun snugging away in his undershorts a little source of chance, reliable frictions to nudge him onward through the workday—anything company-keeping that could be counted on not to slide out of the elasticky leg holes: a half-dollar packet of chocolate tittles, maybe, that was barely noticeable in the baggy surround of the wide-cut trousers so popular at the time.

For by now the woman had at last brought what is usually called the other mouth to within only inches of my lips, but it is not a mouth, obviously, although I let myself go along with the goodwill behind the comparison, the way I will remain loyal to anything deliberately and faithfully misunderstood, and I fussed my tongue against the vital trifles hung inside of her, as much of the curtailed finery as I could find, and gave the whole insimplicity of it a slow-circling, examinational lick, until I was taking a sudden tepid downwash on the tongue.

It was a familiar, latrine indribble that must have tasted, no doubt, like trouble just starting out.

Grateful acknowledgment is made to the editors of the publications in which the entries in this book originally appeared (some in different form and under different titles):

Cimarron Review	"All Told"
Columbia: A Journal of Literature and Art	"Men Your Own Age"
Denver Quarterly	"Leatrice"
Dominion Review	"Meltwater"
Fence	"Her Dear Only Father's Lone Wife's Solitudinized, Peaceless Son"
Fetish: An Anthology	"This Is Nice of You"
Impossible Object	"Dog and Owner"
Mid-American Review	"Carriers"
New York Tyrant	"In Kind"
NOON	"Daught," "Femme," "Fingerache," "I Have to Feel Halved," "I Was in Kilter with Him a Little," "The Least Sneaky of Things," "My Final Best Feature," "People Shouldn't Have to Be the Ones to Tell You," "A Woman with No Middle Name"
Post Road	"Eminence"
The Quarterly	"The Boy," "Chaise Lozenge," "In Case of in No Case," "The Summer I Could Walk Again"
StoryQuarterly	"Heights," "Spills," "Uncle"
Unsaid: A Journal of Difference:	"I Crawl Back to People"

"I Was in Kilter with Him a Little" also appeared in the chapbook *Partial List of People to Bleach* and is reprinted here with permission from Future Tense Books. Thankfulness is extended as well to the editors of the anthologies in which the following pieces have been reprinted: "People Shouldn't Have to Be the Ones to Tell You," in *The Anchor Book of New American Short Stories* (Anchor Books); "Her Dear Only Father's Lone Wife's Solitudinized, Peaceless Son," in *A Best of Fence: The First Nine Years* (Fence Books); "Uncle" and "The Least Sneaky of Things," in *PP/FF: An Anthology* (Starcherone Books).

With deepest gratitude to John Yau, Gordon Lish, Brian Evenson, Ben Marcus, Diane Williams, Fiona Maazel, Kevin Sampsell, Pamela Ryder, Elle Fallon, the National Endowment for the Arts, and the Foundation for Contemporary Arts.

Gary Lutz's other books are *Stories in the Worst Way* (Alfred A. Knopf, 1996; Calamari Press, 2009) and *Partial List of People to Bleach* (Future Tense Books, 2007).

Fifteen hundred copies of I *Looked Alive* were printed and bound at Thomson-Shore in Dexter, Michigan. The book is set in Eric Gill's Johanna, and the display type is Interstate, designed by Tobias Frere-Jones.